MASON

THOMAS PENDLETON

MASON

HARPER TEEN

An Imprint of HarperCollins*Publishers*

HarperTeen is an imprint of HarperCollins Publishers.

Mason

www.harperteen.com

Library of Congress Cataloging-in-Publication Data
Pendleton, Thomas, date.
    Mason / by Thomas Pendleton. — 1st ed.
       p.   cm.
    Summary: When a sadistic high school student tries to cover up a mur-
der by brutally beating an innocent girl, his mentally challenged but psy-
chically gifted brother, Mason, uses his powers to bring about justice in
their sleepy Louisiana town.
    ISBN 978-0-06-117736-1 (pbk.)
    [1. People with mental disabilities—Fiction. 2. Psychic ability—
Fiction. 3.   Brothers—Fiction. 4.   Psychopaths—Fiction. 5.
Louisiana—Fiction. 6. Horror stories.] I. Title.
PZ7.P38413Mas 2008   2007037431
[Fic]—dc22   CIP
                                                                    AC

Typography by Andrea Vandergrift

First Edition

This book is dedicated to
Kristine Dikeman, a wonderful
constant in a changing world.
And, of course, JCP.
You know who you are,
and you know what you did.

ACKNOWLEDGMENTS

This is, at best, an abbreviated list of those whose knowledge, support, and kindness made this book possible. Through encouragement and inspiration, these folks kept the wheels turning: Linda Addison, Pete S. Allen, Laura Arnold, Megan Bulloch, P. D. Cacek, Ellen Datlow, Gerard Houarner, Barbara Lalicki, Dallas Mayr, Mark McLaughlin, Margaret Miller, James A. Moore, Jane Osnovich, and Matt Schwartz.

For their friendship and critical acumen: Daniel Braum, Nicholas Kaufmann, Sarah Langan, K. Z. Perry, and Stefan Petrucha. They all get cake.

PART ONE

1
Preparing the Canvas

On a cold January night, a nine-year-old named Gene Avrett walked down the hall toward his little brother's bedroom. Gene intended to kill the boy, because he wanted to see what it felt like. The idea excited him. His heart tripped fast, like he was on the first plunge of a roller coaster, and his palms were wet with sweat.

Quietly he entered the room and closed the door. As he did, several sheets of paper rustled. They were pinned to the door and each held a picture drawn with crayon, like the ones his mama taped to the fridge. The pictures were stupid—butterflies and flowers and a little girl in a white dress. Silly kid stuff and nothing more.

Gene crossed to the bed and gazed down. Moonlight poured through the window to cover his brother's face, and a small teddy bear rested near his head. His parents called the brat "special." Why they couldn't just call him a retard like everyone else did, Gene didn't know. There he lay in his bed, a bit of drool dripping out of the corner of his mouth. The dummy should have been locked in the attic. Instead, he was treated like a prince.

Gene was sick of it.

Leaning over the bed with his hands outstretched, Gene moved stealthily, as if he were trying to catch a skittish toad. He pinched the boy's nose closed. Then he pressed his palm over his brother's mouth and winced with disgust when the drool touched him. Otherwise, he liked the way it felt—his fingers pressing into the soft, warm skin. A faint pulse played against his fingers. He wondered how long it would take for the heart to stop.

Suddenly his brother's eyes shot open. Gene saw fear in them. He liked that. It made his heart beat even faster, but the thrill ended too soon.

From down the hall rose a terrible cry. The sound, muffled by two closed doors, still was enough to startle Gene. It was his daddy. Gene released the grip on his brother's face and leaped away from the bed.

He rushed to the door and opened it a crack. The hallway stretched before him, shadows on shadows. The door at the end of the hall burst open. His daddy, wearing blue boxer shorts and a white T-shirt stretched tight over his belly, rushed out. He dashed five steps down the corridor and paused by the railing. His eyes were wild. His mouth worked furiously, though he made no sound. He ran his hands through his hair, combing it madly with his fingers.

Then Gene's mama appeared, and Gene knew that his fun was over. She'd be up all night now. She would want to sit with her "special" boy and comfort him. But first she hurried to his daddy's side, grasped his arm, and tried to console him.

Gene's daddy started screaming again, shouting at the top of his lungs. He waved his hands in the air like he was being attacked by a swarm of bees. Of course, Gene had seen his daddy in a state before, but this fit was so bad, he was getting nervous.

Just then Gene saw what his daddy saw. A flock of black birds appeared in the hallway. They came out of nowhere, seeming to form from the shadows to fill Gene's vision. The crows swarmed the narrow corridor and covered the open space above the stairs, but only for a second. *What the hell?* Gene thought. He blinked and rubbed his eyes, and the birds disappeared.

When the brief shock passed, Gene saw his daddy was still there, waving his arms and screaming, but he was alone now. His mama seemed to have vanished completely.

Gene stepped into the hall, but he stopped when his little brother began to cry. It was a dreadful noise, part tears and part choking. He turned toward the sound. Looking at his gross little brother, Gene ground his teeth together.

Tears slid down the boy's face. His hands slapped at the blankets as his cry for "Mama" rose into the darkened room. Behind Gene, his daddy called out. This time the man was forming actual words—something about needing an ambulance—but for the moment, Gene kept his attention on the sobbing brat. . . .

Mama's "special" boy . . .

Mason.

2
We Learn The Shape

Rene Denton sat on the block of concrete, sipping her coffee and watching students enter the school building in groups of two and three and four. Buses lined up on the left, already emptied of their student cargo. Above the double glass doors through which her friends and peers entered was a sign that read MARCHAND HIGH SCHOOL. The same name was carved into the stone slab under her butt. She flipped a lock of blond hair over her ear, took another drink from the cup, and decided the sign made no sense.

High school? It wasn't logical. There was no low school. There was elementary school and then middle school and then high school. Silly. But Rene figured language was pretty loose. After all, they called the cup of coffee she held a "tall," and it was the smallest size the shop sold.

She spent a few more seconds mulling over the sign,

moving letters and words around in meaningless ana-grams. Switched the first letters so that in her mind it read *Harchand Migh School*, and that led her to *Harsh on My School*, which she kind of liked, at least enough to spark a tiny smile.

If her friends knew how much pleasure she took in playing with words and phrases, they would write her off as a total geek. Of course when Cassie or Lorraine (who insisted on being called Lara, like the *Tomb Raider* chick) needed help in English Comp, they came to Rene. At least they had in middle school.

Rene slid off the stone sign and walked across the grass. She paused when she noticed a tall, broad-shouldered boy rushing toward the entrance.

Mason, she thought.

Mason Avrett was a year older than Rene, but as chil-dren they had been best friends. They played tag in the park and chased toads out to the swamps past the Ditch, the rundown part of Marchand where Mason lived with his aunt.

But Rene had grown up, and Mason hadn't. He remained the same sweet kid who liked to play tag and chase toads, while Rene became more interested in clothes and hairstyles and boy bands and television stars. She had inched away from him, drawn to friends like Cassie Ferguson, who knew everything there was to know about personal style, and Lara Pearce, who was like E! Entertainment in heels: able to quote useless facts about every celebrity on the planet.

Rene waited for the school door to close behind Mason before she continued toward the building.

Inside, the hallways were crowded with kids. Some picked through their lockers for books and pens, while others simply stood around talking, waiting for the first bell to ring. On the way to her locker, Rene said hello to her friend Susan, who was nose to nose with Mark Decouteaux. Susan gave Rene a quick glance and said, "Hey," but immediately returned to staring into her boyfriend's eyes.

Ever since those two had met, Rene hardly saw Susan. They used to hang out all the time, but suddenly Susan only had time for Mark.

It was weird and a little depressing the way her friends had changed over the summer. These days, everything felt more intense. Talk of boys. Talk of homework. Talk of life. They were in high school now, and while Rene felt that things weren't totally different—she hung out with most of the same people and still knew most of the kids passing her in the halls—she did admit they weren't the same, either.

Rene thought she understood it. Her friends—not just Susan, Cassie, and Lara, but all of the popular kids—who last year were at the top of the middle-school food chain, now found themselves a few links lower, and the eagerness to win their place in this fresh ecosystem rolled off of them like nasty perfume.

At her locker, Rene spun in the combination and pulled up the handle. She dropped her book bag in with a *clunk*. As she reached up for her English book, loud and grating laughter drew her attention down the hall.

She turned to the noise and thought, *Oh, no*.

Mason stood in the middle of the hallway, looking confused. Three boys had gathered around him and were playing Keep Away with one of his books.

"Hey, 'Tard," Ricky Langham said. "Catch!"

Ricky threw a notebook over Mason's grasping fingers. Lump Hawthorne, a burly kid with a flattop, snagged the notebook. He laughed and shook his head, tossing the book to the side and into the hands of Hunter Wallace, who lifted the notebook high in the air like a trophy and turned in a slow circle, showing it to the kids who'd gathered around them in the hall. Hunter's eyes fell on Rene and his gaze sharpened. He flicked his tongue at her.

Gross, Rene thought. Hunter was such a pig. He was tall and muscular with shaggy black hair and a nasty beard. Tattoos of barbed wire snaked around his forearms and disappeared into the sleeves of his shirt. Everyone knew Hunter was a bully. They also knew he dealt drugs. Though not the scariest guy in school—Mason's older brother, Gene, won that prize—Hunter was a close second.

Hunter tossed the book back to Lump, who held on to it. He opened the notebook and flipped through the pages, walking backward to keep Mason at a distance.

"Nothing in here," Lump said.

"Like his head," Ricky called with a laugh.

Looking desperate, Mason charged after Lump. "It's mine," he said.

Lump closed the book and cocked his arm back, whipping the notebook across the hall like a Frisbee. Ricky caught it.

This is so childish, Rene thought, infuriated by Hunter and his gang's cruelty. She was going to put a stop to this crap. Maybe she and Mason weren't best friends anymore, but she wasn't just going to stand by and watch Hunter humiliate the kid.

She started toward them, but a face on the far side of the skirmish stopped her in mid stride. Gene Avrett leaned against the wall at the end of the hallway. His arms were crossed and he was smiling, amused by the ridicule of his little brother.

The taunts continued and the notebook soared from Hunter to Ricky to Lump. Between them, Mason shuffled desperately, trying to retrieve his pad. He looked so distraught, Rene thought he might burst into tears.

That's enough, she thought.

But before Rene could put a stop to Hunter's mean game, Mason did it himself. He sat down on the linoleum floor with his chin to his chest. He didn't cry the way Rene knew Hunter wanted him to. Instead he just sat there silently staring at the shining floor and the shoes of the boys who tormented him.

Rene looked up at Gene. He shrugged and stepped away from the wall. He turned the corner and disappeared.

Knowing that he wasn't going to have any more fun with Mason, Hunter dropped the notebook and led his gang down the hall. The rest of the kids returned to their conversations or their lockers. They'd wanted a morning smack down to get the day off to an exciting start, and all they got was another example of Hunter's bullying.

Once the other boys were gone, Mason grabbed his notebook. He stood up and walked down the hall with his head low.

Rene felt awful for him. Mason didn't really belong in high school. He was held back two grades in elementary school before his aunt made a deal with the school district to allow him to progress up the educational ladder. Technically, he would not graduate, just as he had not graduated from middle school, but most days Mason seemed to enjoy coming to school.

Still, he suffered for it.

"Did you and Mason ever play Show Me?" Lara Pearce asked before wrapping her lips around the straw jutting from her can of diet cola. Lara's straight black hair fell like curtains on either side of her face when she leaned forward.

"Gross and not even," Rene replied.

They sat outside under the hot Louisiana sun, eating their lunches on the bleachers overlooking the football field. Other kids took up positions along the benches up and down the rows. Next to her, Cassie Ferguson shook her head.

Releasing the straw, Lara said, "But he's like a giant. I'll bet he swings like a horse."

"I can't even believe you'd say that," Cassie whispered, obviously as disturbed by the notion as Rene. "He's mentally challenged, Lara."

"Then he'd be really grateful, wouldn't he?"

"Can we talk about somebody normal?" Cassie said, exasperated.

Rene winced at this remark, figuring Mason was normal enough. It wasn't like he was a freak or anything. He just didn't learn the way other people did. Still, she remained quiet and looked out at the sign draping the far bleachers.

Marchand Water Moccasins.
Warchand Mater Woccasins.

Briefly she wondered if she could pronounce the name of her school's sports teams backward and figured it would be easy enough until she got to *Dnahcram*, which just sounded too complicated and kind of silly, unless she left the D silent and said *Nahcram*, which would be pronounced *Noshrom*. But that was silly too.

"Well, what about Hunter?" Lara said.

"What is your need for freaks?"

"He's hot."

"He's scary," Rene said.

"I like bad boys," Lara replied.

"You know, the reputation you make for yourself in high school will stay with you your entire life," Cassie said, her voice soft and drawn out like the Southern belle she so wanted to become. "If you want to be respected as a lady, you'll respect yourself first."

"Oh, do not burden me with your dinosaur logic," Lara said, swatting at Cassie's hair and sending a few strands out of place. "I know your mama's shoveling that Southern gentility crap into you, but the only thing that kept that fiction alive was isolation. We're wired now. All of that Southern-hospitality-prim-and-proper thinking is dusted."

"So, you're going to be a whore?" Cassie asked.

"I'm expressing my sexual nature," Lara countered with a smile.

"Well, quit expressing it over lunch," Rene said. "There are other things to talk about."

"You wanna talk about homework?"

"What about the carnival next Friday?" Cassie said. "That will be fun."

"Not without dates it won't. A bunch of kiddie rides and games? Please."

Rene listened to her friends bicker and wished Susan still hung out with them. She always had something interesting to talk about. But Susan's halfhearted greeting in the hall that morning was about as deep as things got with her these days.

This is growing up, Rene thought. Susan had let her childhood friends go, like when Rene stopped playing with Mason. Maybe Cassie was wrong. Maybe nothing you built for yourself—even a reputation—stayed with you your whole life. Maybe nothing lasted forever but rather existed in parcels, some large, others far too small, each tossed away when empty. After all, there was no way to move forward if you carried every little thing you'd ever acquired with you. You'd get bogged down and crushed by them. Things had to be tossed out.

She looked across the football field. On the far bleachers, Mason sat alone, eating a sandwich, drinking from a juice box and every now and then looking up at the sky. He caught her looking his way and held up a big hand. He waved furiously.

Rene lifted her hand, then turned back to her friends.

3
Palette

Mason watched in wide-eyed awe as his teacher brought Mickey Mouse to the classroom by drawing just a few circles on the chalkboard. Immediately, he lowered his head and copied the image on his own paper. His accomplishment—in addition to the sight of his favorite cartoon character—made him grin so hard his cheeks hurt.

Wedged in the desk that was too small for him, Mason snapped his head up, away from the wonderful mouse on his notepaper, back to the board to see what new and amazing things Mrs. Denver would create. Mason had always liked to draw, but Gene told him he wasn't very good at it and that people didn't like his drawings. Gene had told him to stop it, and Mason had, for a very long time. But now, Mrs. Denver, his teacher, wanted him and the rest of the class to draw, and Mason knew you always did what your teachers told you to do. Aunt Molly said it was "a must."

In the seat ahead of his, Hunter Wallace was making faces at Julia Landry. The boy with the funny lines painted on his arms flicked his tongue in the air, and his bearded face scrunched in an ugly way. Julia dropped her head and stared at the paper in front of her. In her chair by the window, Lara Pearce stared at Hunter and Julia. To Mason she looked sleepy as she chewed on the end of her pencil. When Lara caught him looking, her eyes got really wide for a second and she looked away.

"Now, I know these exercises may seem rudimentary to some of you," Mrs. Denver said. "But by utilizing simple geometric shapes, you'll learn perspective, depth of field, and negative space, while building a strong foundation for your future artistic endeavors."

On the green chalkboard, Mrs. Denver drew a square and then another, smaller square, and in no time, Mason found himself looking at a nice little house with a chimney and smoke rolling like fluffy clouds up the surface of the blackboard. The house looked a little like his aunt Molly's house, but the picture on the board didn't have a porch.

"Hunter," Mrs. Denver warned, catching the boy in mid tongue flick. "Why don't you come up and show the class your talent instead of showing them your foolishness?"

Hunter threw back his head in defiance. Next to him, Julia turned bright red and covered her mouth to keep the giggles inside. The rest of the class laughed. Mason didn't know why everybody was laughing, but he liked to laugh, so he did. Hunter spun around and fixed a mean look on Mason, who dropped his eyes back to the notepad and the happy cartoon mouse he'd drawn there.

"You don't laugh at me," Hunter whispered. "You don't never laugh at me."

"Hunter," Mrs. Denver said.

"Mason said he wants to go first."

Hearing his name, Mason looked up in confusion. Did he do something wrong? Was he supposed to do something? He searched the faces of his classmates and the face of his teacher for answers.

"I think Mason is able to speak for himself," Mrs. Denver said, giving him a warm glance. "Would you like to draw for us, Mason?"

Now the whole class was looking at him, and some were still laughing. A hot flush rose on his cheeks. Mrs. Denver lifted a piece of chalk from the tray and pointed it in his direction.

"S'pose," Mason said, already prying himself out

between the chair and the desk.

Julia Landry stared at him like he had a bug on his face, and Hunter Wallace smirked. Embarrassed, Mason walked to the front of the class with his head bowed. He took the dusty stick of chalk from Mrs. Denver and asked, "What am I s'posed to do?"

The class broke up with fresh laughter, their shrill voices slicing the air like a dozen shards of glass to slash Mason's stomach. Now he didn't feel embarrassed so much as afraid.

"Just draw a house," Mrs. Denver said in a quiet, comforting voice. "You don't even have to draw the same house I did. You can draw your own house if you like."

But when Mason turned away from his teacher, chalk in hand, and faced the freshly erased chalkboard, a different picture came into his mind. He saw a big house with a lot of curlicues and a pointed tower and really neat pillars in the front. Mason touched the board with his chalk, and the lines and shadows of the big Victorian home in his mind slipped onto the dark green surface before him. He began to trace them.

Lost in the lines, Mason forgot Mrs. Denver and the class full of students sitting behind him. He felt as if he'd been pulled out of the classroom and dropped into the front yard of this pretty house with the curlicues and the front door open in welcome.

When he finished the picture, he did not look at it. He looked back at the other kids in the class, and he looked at Mrs. Denver to see how he'd done, because it was important to do well on assignments since he didn't do so good on tests. His classmates and his teacher wore matching expressions of disbelief, and Mason felt certain he'd done something wrong.

His cheeks burned—physically burned—as he put the chalk back in the tray. His head lower than it had been when he walked to the front of the class, he started to walk back to his chair.

"Mason," Mrs. Denver said. She grasped his shoulder and made him look at her. When he did, he was surprised to see her smiling. "Where did you learn to draw like that?"

He chewed on his lower lip, not quite understanding what Mrs. Denver meant. She turned him slowly toward the blackboard, but even as he saw the drawing, he didn't see it as something he created. The picture was in his head and then on the board, and he just traced it.

"It's exquisite," Mrs. Denver said. From the back of the class, Hunter Wallace made a farting noise, and she shot him a warning with her eyes. "But where did you learn this?"

"It's just a picture," Mason told her.

"Will you stay after class?" Mrs. Denver asked.

"Am I in trouble?"

"No, Mason, you're not in trouble. You may take your seat now."

Once the other students had filed out and Mason Avrett was left alone in her classroom, Charlotte Denver closed the door. She could tell Mason was uncomfortable and she knew her best approach was to be direct, so that he didn't unduly worry himself.

"I'd like you to draw some things for me." She put a sketch pad and a sharpened pencil on Mason's desk. Taking the seat next to his, she thought for a moment and asked him to draw a dog, a man, and a boat.

"All at once?"

"You can draw them on separate pages if you like."

Mason lowered his head and stared at the sheet of blank paper before him as if expecting to see something push its way through the page. Then his eyes went blank, and his hand started to move quickly.

He doesn't even know I'm here, Charlotte Denver thought, watching Mason frantically scribble over the page. *He gets lost in it; the picture consumes him.*

When Mason finished, Charlotte took the drawing from him and was again amazed. The dog he drew was a sleek golden retriever suspended in midair as if to catch a ball. Never in all of her years of teaching had she seen such precision. The depth of form was perfect, as was the rendering of the animal's fur. Looking at the image, she felt her stomach roll because it looked like the dog might actually jump off the page to land in her lap.

"That's Lightning," Mason said. "He was my best friend until he ran away."

"I'm sorry he ran away, Mason," she told him, still transfixed by how he had brought the lines and smudges of pencil lead to life. "Can you draw a man for me?"

"What man?"

"Any man you think of."

This request seemed to confound Mason, but Charlotte wasn't surprised. He was just overwhelmed. She would have asked Mason to draw his daddy, but he didn't have one. The boy lived with his single aunt and an older brother. His daddy was gone, mama too.

Charlotte Denver remembered Mason's father, Nelson. His absence was probably the best thing that could have happened to the boy. The man was unstable. Oh, he'd been a looker when he was young, but even then, folks knew something wasn't quite right with the man. For years, Nelson Avrett had been seen talking to himself or laughing uncontrollably or gaping in awe at people for no apparent reason. He was crazy as a rat in a bell jar—that was certain. Still, everyone in town was shocked to hear he'd killed his wife.

Thinking about Nelson Avrett, Charlotte was reminded of her own father, his anger and his fists. The memories made her shiver.

Better to just look at the wonderful drawing of the dog, or back at the blackboard to see how beautifully Mason had sketched the house. From this distance, she noticed that the Victorian architecture, even the ginger-bread patterns that Mason had created, were exactly like those of her own house.

Isn't that something? she thought. Maybe he knew where she lived and drew the place from memory to please her.

"I don't know him," Mason said, tearing the sheet from the sketchbook. "He looks scary and mean. I didn't want him to be mean, but he is."

Charlotte attempted to laugh off Mason's anxiety, but the smile died on her face and a terrible weight settled in her chest when she saw the picture. She followed the cruel brow and the piercing eyes, flinched at the sight of the balled fists, and choked back a sob as she remembered vile words spewing from a hateful man's screaming mouth.

Her father stared back at her from the page.

Outside the Lines

A lot of Rene's friends complained about Marchand being too small, but she liked it well enough. She imagined she would go off to college and maybe find a job in another city far away. Once she graduated high school, she might never live in this town again, and that was okay, even a little exciting, but she certainly didn't think Marchand was the cesspool of boredom many of her classmates called it.

She walked along Main Street. The evening air felt good on her face.

Her parents were way quiet over dinner, which meant they were about to have a fight. It happened about once a month, and when Rene saw the signs, she got out of the house. She didn't worry about it, because her parents' arguments never lasted long. Tomorrow everything would be fine and normal again.

For now, she walked down Main Street, peeking into the shop fronts. Some were already decorated for Halloween, which was still more than a month away. On either side of brightly colored cardboard witch and jack-o'-lantern faces, she noticed the familiar merchandise on the shops' shelves. Toasters and shovels gleamed in the window of Marchand Hardware; laptop computers sat on pedestals in the window of the Tech Smart; a dark painting of a creepy hillside hung on a partial wall at the front of Gallery North.

Rene took comfort in the familiar. Even her parents' arguments were something of a comfort because they were so predictable and short-lived.

Two boys with long hair passed her on the sidewalk. They weren't old enough to go to Marchand High, but they dressed like a lot of the kids there, and both eyed her sheepishly before hurrying past. They would be cute in a few years, she thought, but for now they still had the eager faces of children.

Seeing them reminded her of another boy though. A boy she *had* thought cute: Carter Dane. Carter was a tall, dark-haired boy with beautiful skin. He used to go to school with her. He was a straight-A student who always seemed distracted, his eyes often looking sad. Rene had crushed on him for two years, even when she was dating other boys. He just looked so thoughtful and intense.

Earlier in the year, during spring break, Carter had died in a boating accident. The news had shocked Rene to the point she didn't believe it when her mother told her. Rene went to the funeral. She cried and prayed and felt empty for two months—all for a boy she'd only said hi to in the halls.

Since then, Rene had found herself weighing other boys against her memory of Carter. None of them could compete, of course. This one was too short. This one was goofy. This one belched in the caf'. To Rene, they were just boys. She'd found her prince, and he had died tragically. Who could follow that?

"Hello, Rene."

The voice startled Rene badly, and she jumped a little. She hadn't realized someone was walking so close.

Placing a hand over her chest to quell the rapid *tip-tap* of her heart, Rene turned. There stood Mason's older brother, Gene. The sight of him amplified her quickened pulse, making it sound like thunder in her ears.

"Oh hi, Gene," she said with a trembling voice.

"Did I scare you?"

Yes, Rene thought, *you always scare me.*

25

Gene Avrett was a few inches taller than Rene. He kept his hair short and neatly styled. He wore a gray silk T-shirt over fashionably distressed black jeans. Gene always smiled, but unlike his brother's sweet and child-like grin, Gene's humor came from a much darker place, never touching his eyes, which were as clear and blue and toxic as window cleaner.

"I'm so very sorry," Gene said in a voice slow and measured. The words seemed to slither from his lips.

That was another creepy thing about Gene—the way he spoke. He was only three years older than Rene, but he tried to act so grown up and sophisticated. It was like he was trying to be superior to everyone.

"It's okay," she said.

"Were you headed to Frank's?" Gene asked.

"Yes," Rene lied. She wished she hadn't answered so quickly, because it showed how scared she was, but it was too late to take it back. "Yes, I'm meeting friends."

Though people passed them on the sidewalk and she stood right out in the open, Rene felt alone with Gene, like he'd locked them in a room far from help and hope and saving. Her skin pimpled with unease, and she turned away from him to look down the sidewalk.

"Then we'll walk together," Gene told her. "That's the very place I was headed myself."

"Um . . . oh . . . okay."

Frank's was only a block down, but it looked miles

away with Gene at her side. Rene kept her eyes on the sidewalk, occasionally casting glances at the pedestrians who passed, wanting them to see her.

"Have you seen little Mason lately?" Gene asked.

"No," Rene said. "Well, at school. I see him at school sometimes."

"Isn't it wonderful how they allow him to pretend to be normal?"

Rene clenched her jaw and nodded her head.

"It's really quite progressive of them. I mean, not long ago, they would have locked someone like him up in an asylum or used him as the village idiot. I can't help but think you did the right thing . . . freezing him out the way you did."

"I didn't freeze him out," Rene said uncertainly, a twinge of guilt sliding into the knot of fear tightening in her stomach.

"Of course you didn't," Gene said. "My mistake. Whatever happened, it was for the best."

Rene heard something unsavory in Gene's tone. She had no interest in what he had to say, but he kept talking anyway.

"Someone like Mason isn't really in control of himself. It isn't his fault, but that doesn't make it right, you know? I mean, when he used to draw pictures of you, they were very nice. You were both just children, and certain thoughts never entered his mind. But children grow. Their bodies change, even if their minds are slow and can't keep up. Hormones and all."

Rene saw where Gene was going with his comments and wanted to scream at him to stop. She remembered the pictures Mason used to draw of her. They were nice. She hadn't really appreciated them then.

Weird, though. Last night on the phone, Lara had mentioned something that had happened in her art class, but Rene hadn't really been paying attention. Something about Mason. Something about a house. It didn't matter. Gene was just being cruel the way Gene was always cruel.

"Mason's a great guy" was all she managed to say.

"I'm glad you think so, and I'm certainly glad you don't have to see the pictures he draws of you now. A young lady should never have to view such filth."

Disgusted, she looked at Gene, who smiled innocently as if he waited for the answer to a simple question. Her anger went a long ways to loosening the knot of fear.

"Good night, Gene," Rene said.

"Aren't you coming in?" He reached out and grabbed the chrome handle of the door. "Won't your friends be waiting?"

"They'll understand," Rene told him, turning away.

Through the window of Frank's she saw Lara, standing at the end of the counter with several boys. She held a glass in her hand, a straw clamped between her lips. Lara blinked and looked away from the tallest of the boys, and then looked back at him through her eyelashes.

She was flirting, and that wouldn't have been bad, except that Lara was flirting with Hunter Wallace. For a moment, Rene thought about charging into Frank's and saving her friend from making a huge mistake, but she felt Gene staring at her, knew he was still holding the door open behind her.

Rene shuddered, cast another look at her stupid friend—*Lara, what are you doing?*—and then walked quickly down the sidewalk.

Gene appreciated the fact that he was feared; it proved the lame-ass hicks in this town were smarter than he had thought. They *should* be afraid of him, and not just because he knew how to throw down a hurt. In fact, that was the least of it. Considering the things he'd pulled off over the years without having spent so much as a blink of time in juvie or jail, he figured his mind was far more dangerous to the fine folks of Marchand than his fists, his knife, or his Beretta 9 mm.

Not that he was above violence. Only a handful of years ago, he was sitting in a coffeehouse out by the college and calmly listening while a couple of frat boys gave him a hard time. Gene's eyes twinkled as he laughed. He even bought his hecklers a round of cappuccinos and wished them a good night before excusing himself from the establishment.

Despite the smile on his face and the twinkle in his eyes, the comedic comments and the amity of friendly raps on the back, Gene's temper shrank and grew tight, coiled like a snake. Even as he freed a twenty from his wallet to buy the college boys their coffee, his thoughts were over an hour into the future, out in the hot air of the parking lot.

He beat two of them unconscious with a tire iron. The third lost an eye. They all lived, but not one of them talked. He'd made it clear enough what would happen if they did.

That had worked out really well for him.

He knew it was all about appearances. You showed your happy face to the world and kept the nastiness hidden in shadows where it belonged. And Gene never bragged about his business. No way. You talk and it sinks you.

Besides, his reputation got around just fine without him saying a word. Seeing the scared face of a kid like Rene Denton was all the proof he needed of that. Hell, he stood at the front of Frank's now and saw a room full of the same fearful expressions. It gave him a good charge.

After catching Hunter Wallace's eye, Gene walked

to the back of the restaurant and through a narrow alley to the men's room. He checked the stall and then stood at the urinal waiting. Two minutes later, Wallace walked through the door. Without saying a word, he handed Gene a wad of cash wrapped in a piece of yellow legal paper. In return, Gene handed Wallace two plain envelopes. Then he stopped to wash his hands at the sink.

"You got yourself a problem," Wallace said, pushing up close to the urinal.

"Do I?" Gene asked, soaping his palms. "How so?"

"Dusty's got himself a new skank, and they've been holed up for the last week, going through product."

Gene dried his hands thoroughly, reached into his pocket, pulled a fifty-dollar bill free of his money clip and handed it to Wallace. A tattooed forearm shot out and snagged the bill, shoved it deep in a pocket.

Gene left the restroom, his thoughts turning darker. He walked into the restaurant and sat in a booth, staring out the window at the parade of hicks.

"You hungry?" the waitress asked, eyeing Gene suspiciously.

He gave her one of his biggest smiles and said, "Indeed. What's good tonight?"

5
Creating Shadows

Mason lay in bed, staring at the wall. Outside, the moon was bright and cast ghostly light through his open window. Even though it was late in the evening and late in the year, it was still very warm. He had pushed his covers away, and they formed a low ridge at the end of his bed. Above this ridge shadows climbed his wall toward the dark ceiling. Long lines from tree branches and dull smudges from the toys he kept on the windowsill formed imperfect shapes against the purplish screen of his bedroom wall, and Mason grinned as he rearranged the shapes with his mind, giving them finer definition and greater detail.

He bent and folded the shadows and realigned them to resemble a house like the one he'd drawn in class for Mrs. Denver. She was nice and liked his pictures. At least she was nice until he drew that angry man.

Mason didn't know who the angry man was, but he upset Mrs. Denver. She made him stop drawing then and told him he could go home. Even though he'd wanted to go home, he felt bad because Mrs. Denver looked so upset. He should have drawn a nice man, a smiling man.

Not a shouting man who waved his fists.

He stared at the shadow-house on the wall. The peaked turret on the left made him think of castles. He knew all about castles. The fairy tales his mama read him when he was little all had castles.

Mason thought hard and shifted the shadows and the light until he imagined a castle painted on his wall. A silhouette leaned out from high in a tower, and he knew this was the princess (because fairy tales always had princesses in castles). Finally, he concentrated on a blob of shadow cast by a small wooden horse. This he elongated and made fierce with a long beak filled with sharp teeth and the impression of thin leathery wings: a dragon.

Mason smiled at the shadow picture on his wall. It reminded him of a long time ago, before his mama and daddy went away. He could almost feel his mother sitting on the bed next to him, could almost smell the sweet scent of chocolate chip cookies, which she'd fix in the evening so he had snacks for the next day.

"*Once upon a time,*" her voice whispered to him.

His bedroom door opened, startling Mason. The wall picture fell apart, reduced to simple dark smudges amid the moonlight. Mason turned his head and saw his brother, Gene, closing the door.

"We've had a bad day," Gene whispered.

A flare of panic shot through Mason's belly and lodged in his chest. His brother only visited at night to punish him. He struggled to remember what he had done wrong. He looked at the sock hanging from Gene's fist. It bulged like the body of a white snake devouring a rat. Only there were two bulges, like the snake had had dinner twice. But thoughts of snakes quickly faded as Mason searched for some event, no matter how minor, in the course of the day that might have angered Gene. Because Gene must be angry with him.

"I didn't do anything," Mason whispered.

"Didn't you?" Gene asked. "How can you be sure? Your head is broken. Are you absolutely certain you didn't do anything wrong?"

"Yes, Gene. Yes. I didn't do anything. I didn't." But Mason wasn't sure. Maybe he *had* done something wrong. He didn't know what it was. He never knew what might make Gene angry.

Just don't, Gene. Please don't.

"If you didn't do anything wrong," Gene asked, "then why am I here? Don't you think I'd rather be asleep? Don't you think there are a hundred other things I'd rather be doing?"

"I s'pose, but I didn't do anything." Still, Gene's logic worked into Mason's thoughts. His brother wouldn't just hit him for the sake of hitting him. That made no sense at all. People didn't do that, especially family. There must be a reason, and if Mason could just remember what he'd done, he could apologize and promise to never do it again.

"I keep trying to teach you," Gene said, stepping into the room. The lumpy sock swung against his thigh as he walked. "I want you to learn and be a normal person, but you just won't learn."

"I will," Mason said quickly, scooting back on the mattress until his back hit the wall. "I'm sorry, I'll try."

Just don't, Gene.

"You always say you'll try, but here I am, having to teach you all over again."

Gene stepped into the moonlight. He didn't look angry, but then Gene never looked angry. He always looked like he was remembering a joke.

"You know stealing is wrong," Gene said. "Stealing is a sin, Mason."

"I didn't steal."

"Didn't you? Do you know what stealing is?"

"Taking someone else's things, but I didn't take anything."

"And yet, something of mine is gone. It's gone forever. Now, is that fair?"

Mason didn't answer. The threads of his thoughts were tangled, and he tried to work his way through them, but having Gene standing near the bed with the sock thumping against his leg, looking like he'd heard a funny joke, just tangled the knots more.

"Is that fair?" Gene repeated.

"No," Mason said.

"That's right. It's not fair. And someone's got to take responsibility. Someone's got to step up. That's what normal people do. That's what good people do."

"But . . ." Mason tried.

"Ah-ah," Gene replied, holding up his hand to interrupt Mason's protests. "Someone's got to step up."

Terror shot like flashing lights in Mason's head. Already confused, he was unable to follow the fragments his mind produced: *I didn't steal. Punishment. Don't, Gene. Please. Didn't steal. Mama, make him stop. Didn't. Step up.*

Then his thoughts shut down completely. His body went numb.

As he'd done too many times to count, Mason slid out of bed and turned. He dropped slowly to the floor and sat cross-legged with his back to Gene. He reached his arms out and laid them on the bed. He lowered his head, awaiting his punishment.

The stuffed sock came down hard on his shoulder blades. It felt like two fists punching him, but Mason didn't make a sound. Another blow rang pain all up and down his back, but Mason didn't say a word. Eyes closed, he saw nothing but a field of black. Behind him, Gene continued to speak, but in those moments of anguish, the words meant nothing to Mason.

Dusty. Loser. Skank. Profits. MY money. Dusty.

Gotta step up.

Someone has GOT to step up.

Gene stayed longer than usual. The punishment was so bad that Mason couldn't keep hiding in his mind. Tears spilled from his eyes, and his lips trembled as he tried to keep from crying out. He thought it would never end—thought he'd done something so wrong Gene would kill him for it.

Then it stopped. Mason's back throbbed with a dozen painful hearts, all beating miserably against his skin. His hands were clenched into tight fists. Sweat poured over his face, his neck, and his wounded back.

"There," Gene said, out of breath, "now, don't you feel better?"

Mason said nothing.

"Be sure you keep a shirt on around Molly for the next week."

Mason sat trembling.

"Did you hear me?"

"I'spose."

Finally, Gene left the room, and Mason got to his feet.

Mason lay on his stomach. He looked through a film of tears at the door to his room. More than anything, he wanted his mama to walk through that door. She'd know how to make the pain stop. She'd bring him cookies and kiss his forehead and stroke his hair. Maybe she'd tell him a story to take his mind off the pain.

So hard did he wish to see his mother, she appeared in the room before him. A green cotton dress hung from her shoulders and hugged her waist tight. She was still really pretty. Her long brown hair hung straight to her shoulders. Her face was shaped like a valentine heart, and she smiled at him.

She flickered and almost disappeared, but Mason concentrated harder, until she looked as solid as the chair by the door. With a bit more thought, he gave her motion, brought her close to his bedside, and made her sit next to him.

The scent of sweet chocolate-chip cookies filled the air.

His mama reached out the way he wanted her to, but he didn't feel her palm on his brow. It was just a mind picture, and mind pictures couldn't touch you.

Seeing her would have to be enough.

"I didn't do anything," Mason whispered.

His mama nodded her head and smiled a little wider, even though her eyes looked sad. Her lips moved, but no sound came out. His mind pictures couldn't talk, either, but he knew what she'd say.

You're my special boy. My good boy.

"Are you ever coming home?"

I am home.

"But for real?"

Mama shook her head. *No.*

"I miss you," he said. "Lots."

I miss you. . . .

His bedroom door opened again, but Mason was so happy, he barely noticed. He wanted to keep looking at his mama's pretty smile and her warm, sad eyes.

"What the hell?" Gene whispered.

The voice startled Mason. Panic flared again. His thoughts became jumbled.

No more, Gene.

I'll learn. I'll learn.

I'll step up.

The mind picture of his mama disappeared.

"Who . . . ?" But Gene couldn't finish the thought. He stood in the open doorway. Even from his bed across the room, Mason could see the door trembling in his big brother's grip.

Did Gene see Mama too? Mason wondered. He wanted to ask, but he was too afraid to say anything.

From the darkened threshold, Gene chuckled. He stepped back into the hall, whispering, "I must be losing it."

He closed the door without saying another word.

He did see her, Mason thought. *He did.*

6
Chiaroscuro

On Thursday morning, Rene woke very early to the sound of rain. The night before had been clear with a big orange moon in the sky, but sometime during the early-morning hours, the clouds had rolled in. She opened her eyes to the gray downpour smearing the world beyond her window. She blinked and rolled over, giving herself an extra five minutes of pillow time. Her bed was just too comfortable to leave, and it was Friday, and there were surely a dozen other good excuses to lie there and do nothing.

Maybe a sick day was in order. She could always fake a stomachache. Hold a thermometer near the lightbulb of her desk lamp. Just stay in her comfortable bed all day, watching *Smallville* or *Heroes* on DVD. Once her mom went to work, she could get online and text some friends or just surf 'n' shop the web.

41

As tempting as these thoughts were, Rene rolled out of bed. She scratched her head. Yawned. Walked to the bathroom to shower. No hooky today.

There was a test on the colonies in American history class.

They were choosing lab partners in chem, and if she missed it, she'd end up with Eric Crawford or Donnie Langham or some other slacker who'd make Rene do all the work.

Plus, Lara needed a talking-to.

All night Rene had worried about her friend. Lara had actually gone out on a date with Hunter Wallace. It seemed like a repulsive impossibility, but Cassie had told her all about it on the phone last night. Rene had been grossed out just seeing Lara flirt with the boy on Tuesday night, but dating? The idea was sickening. Her friend might have had a thing for bad boys, but Hunter wasn't just bad. He was dangerous. Maybe not as dangerous as Gene Avrett, but not far off. They were two sides of the same coin. Gene was heads. Hunter was tails.

Maybe that's why he's such an ass, Rene thought. She smiled at the notion, but it quickly faded. Hunter wasn't a guy you joked about. Everyone knew Hunter kept a gun in the glove box of his car. He'd shown it to enough kids to take the idea out of the realm of school mythology and make it a piece of cold reality. Lara had no business getting mixed up with him.

Turning on the hot water, Rene decided to call Lara. They could meet for coffee. It was kind of early, but it would give them a chance to talk without a ton of kids around.

She had to say something.

Rene sat in the coffee shop, already a third of the way through her cappuccino with the remnants of a biscotti dusting the plate beside her. The main room of the coffee shop was pretty cool. Taking its inspiration from Planet Hollywood, the shop walls were covered in classic movie posters—*Casablanca*, *King Kong*, *Citizen Kane*, *The African Queen*. Rene had seen only a couple of the films on television. She often thought about renting some of the others, but watching people who she knew were dead, chatting and smoking and acting like they didn't have a single care in the world, bothered her.

And where the hell was Lara? Her friend promised to meet her before classes, but she was already half an hour late. Rene shook her head and sipped her coffee.

She had met Lara in the sixth grade. Back then Lara was so quiet, so shy. She kept her hair long and straight, like curtains behind which she could hide her face when the world got scary. In fact, Rene's first memory of Lara was of a girl without a face. She'd walked into class, nervous herself because of the new school year, and she saw Lara at her desk, head lowered and face hidden by long, flat sheets of black hair. The hair was clean and shimmered, but the way it covered her features looked so strange.

Mr. Foster had arranged the room, and Rene found herself sitting right next to Lorraine Pearce, who would later insist on being called Lara. They were not immediate friends; that took some time. Over the course of the first month of school, Lara made quiet wise-ass comments when Mr. Foster lectured, and Rene couldn't help but smile at them. Later, they chatted over lunch and at recess. Two other girls, Cassandra Ferguson and Susan Melvoin, joined them, and before the Thanksgiving break, Rene and her new best friends became inseparable. They remained that way for years.

Over the summer, everything changed, though. Susan got involved with Mark Decoteaux, and Lara had what she called "an affair" with a college boy that lasted through most of June. Just before the Fourth of July, when they were all going to go to the river to see the fireworks, the boy bailed town, went back to Alexandria, and never called Lara again. She was crushed and called Rene twenty times a day to talk through her disappointment and hurt.

Rene understood. Lara's parents were almost non-existent. Her dad was a consultant, and he spent more time on planes than he did at home. Her mother was another unrepentant workaholic, and though her office was in the house, she kept herself locked inside it most days, communicating with Lara through email and text messages, even if her daughter was only a room away.

When the boy broke up with her, Lara said it felt like "hanging off the side of a building and having another finger stepped on."

Now this Hunter Wallace situation. Ugh. If that college boy had stepped on one of Lara's fingers, Hunter would stomp his black boot down on her whole hand.

Rene took another sip of coffee and noticed she was rapidly reaching the bottom of the cup. She was about to pull out her cell phone to call Lara, but her friend finally appeared in the doorway.

Lara wore a black string tank over blue jeans. She looked seriously exhausted as she wandered through the shop and dropped into the chair across from Rene.

"Don't even start the disappointed-mama lecture. I am so not in the mood."

"I wasn't going to lecture."

"Yes, you were," Lara said. "I saw it in your eyes when I walked through the door. But I already got my fill of life lessons from Melanie, so my quota has been met."

Melanie was Lara's mother. Rene was always thrown off when Lara called her parents by their first names. Rene couldn't imagine calling her parents Lorelei and Phil. Of course, Cassie called her parents "ma'am" and "sir," which was really weird too.

"What happened?" Rene asked.

"I was trying to get out of the house this morning, and she texted me about some BS that threw my happy in the furnace. Apparently, I have a curfew now."

"A curfew?"

"Yeah," Lara said. She snatched Rene's cup and drained the remaining coffee from it. "I mean, it's like I see my parents every eighth day and on national holidays. They so don't keep track of what's going on, and that's cool. But last night, Melanie decided to put on her mama-crown and got up in my grill about being out too late. And I'm all, too late for what? It's not like they ever said, 'You have to be home by ten or no allowance, young lady.' It's all so stupid."

"How late were you out?"

"Like midnight."

"On a school night?"

"Chill out, Mary Poppins. I wasn't doing anything. I was just out."

"With Hunter?"

Lara broke into a broad smile and looked up from the empty coffee cup. "Yeah. Hot, right?"

"Hardly," Rene replied, despite knowing Lara wasn't going to like it.

But Lara didn't seem upset at all. "You just don't get him."

"That's true enough. I don't get some slacker who deals drugs and carries a gun."

Lara laughed and flipped her hair back. "See, that's what I'm talking about. Hunter doesn't deal. He just lets people say it because it makes him sound like a badass."

"Lara, he does deal, and you know it."

"Fine. So maybe he pimps Tina for some spending cash. So what? Most of us were choking down Ritalin when we were six. We're a chemical generation. Why should we let the adults take all the profits?"

"That's Hunter talking."

"Whatevs," Lara said. "I like him. He's hot."

"He's dangerous."

"That's what makes him hot." She giggled loudly.

"Lara, you shouldn't . . ."

"Oh hell no," Lara interrupted. She lifted a hand and showed Rene the palm. "I told you, no lectures. It's too early, and I am wholly decaffeinated. So, if you want to buy me a latte, I might let you frown at me, but you keep the *shoulds* and *shouldn'ts* in the original packaging. I so can't deal with them right now."

"Okay," Rene said with a sigh. "Fine."

But she couldn't help imagining her friend hanging from the side of a building with Hunter Wallace glaring down on her as he positioned his boot over Lara's clutching fingers.

The morning rain had left a clean coolness in the air. Rene sat alone on the bleachers at lunchtime, staring over the empty football field. Other kids sat higher up or farther down, but Cassie was going to be late and Lara was a no-show. Their conversation had bothered Rene all morning, and now that she didn't have the distraction of teachers and classmates, Rene found herself running their chat over in her head. She should have tried harder to show Lara exactly how bad dating Hunter was. Bad for her head and her heart. Bad for her reputation. But it was futile. Lara did what Lara wanted to do.

Mason appeared on the far side of the field, walking across the concrete at the base of the visitors' bleachers. Rene hadn't seen him since Tuesday morning, and she'd thought he was out sick. His shoulders were slumped, and his steps were slow and seemed pained. He took one step up the stairs and then paused. His hand went to his back, and he leaned forward like an old man. He looked left and right, like he was totally confused, and then he climbed several more steps, hand still on his back. At the first landing, he stopped and sat down clumsily, facing away from

Rene. Facing the wrong direction.

Mason's obvious confusion and pain tore a line of sympathy across Rene's chest.

He shouldn't be at school, she thought. *And he shouldn't be in that house.*

Even though Mason's aunt Molly owned the house, Rene knew that Gene ran it. Molly was a sweet woman who was way too meek to manage a creep like Gene, and Rene couldn't think of a more terrible place for Mason. He should be someplace where people appreciated him.

Sadly, Rene knew, there was no such place. The world wasn't built for people like Mason.

"Afternoon, darlin'," Cassie said just as her shadow fell over Rene.

"Hey," she replied. "What did Mr. Chambers want?"

"Why, he wanted to marry me so that I could carry his children."

"Did he want anything that wasn't illegal?"

"It was just a student-teacher meeting," Cassie said, taking her seat on the bench next to Rene. "As you know, I'm brilliant. He just wanted to let me know it hadn't gone unnoticed. What are you doing?"

"Lunch," Rene said simply, unsure if she should discuss Lara's recent exhibition of bad taste or not.

"Well, you look like your mama packed a tongue sandwich in that bag."

Rene smiled and shook her head. "Nothing that gross."

"I heard you talked to our girl, Lara, about her wholly questionable association with Hunter. I understand it was a total waste of breath."

"It was. Did Lara tell you?"

"Yes. Third period. She was oh-so-thrilled to tell me about her encounter with Hunter last night, and her subsequent grounding."

"She's grounded?" Rene asked, feeling betrayed. "She told me she just had a curfew."

"Indeed," replied Cassie. "I dare say, our sweet Lara is growing into one shady woman. She's making us all look bad. She might as well go all the way into Scaryville and hook up with that lunatic Gene Avrett."

"Don't even say that," Rene said.

"I see his little brother is still at the peak of together." Cassie nodded her head toward Mason, sitting on the bleachers.

It's like he doesn't want to be seen, Rene thought, gazing at Mason's wide back. "Why do you have to pick on him?"

"Sorry. That whole family is just scary."

"He's a nice boy," Rene countered. "You shouldn't slam him just because he doesn't fit into your cotillion fantasy."

"On one hand, I completely agree with you," Cassie

said coolly. "On the other hand . . . ewww!"

"Whatever."

"We all know the way the world should be," Cassie continued. "We also know it's a total fantasy. At some point you have to clue into the fact that life isn't an Amanda Bynes film."

"Maybe. Sometimes I really envy Mason, because he never has to deal with it. I mean, he sees it happening but it doesn't register, right? The rest of us have to watch everything around us turn to crap. All of the pretty shiny things get dark and nasty."

"And then we die," Cassie said, too happily. "Welcome to the meaning of life."

"It blows," Rene said. "So, are we going to the Autumn Carnival tomorrow?"

"Of course we are," Cassie said excitedly. "Eric Crawford asked if I was going to be there."

"I didn't know you liked Eric."

"I don't know if I do yet."

"But you think he's hot?"

"*Everyone* thinks he's hot," Cassie said. "And now that he's rid himself of Miranda Bocage, he's fair game."

"Ugh, Miranda." Rene groaned. Miranda was a pretentious blonde whose father owned a chicken-processing plant that provided chicken to half the fast food chains in the South. She was rich and spoiled and full-on plastic. At seventeen, she'd already had her nose done and had gotten a boob job over the last Christmas holiday—like nobody would notice her jumping from an A-cup to a C-cup in, like, two weeks.

"*Ugh* is right," Cassie said. "I'm just glad Eric snapped out of her evil spell."

"So, should we connect with Lara?"

"Not if she's slumming around with Hunter. I am so not hanging with him. There isn't enough antibacterial soap in the world."

Rene laughed. "I'll talk to her. We'll take her to the mall and have an intervention."

Cassie rolled her eyes. "What she needs is an exorcism."

7
Exhibition

The Autumn Carnival was a two-night celebration, held at Marchand's Riverfront Park. The park was, of course, bordered on one side by the river. On the opposite edge, a steep slope of grass rolled up to Main Street. In between were vast lawns and concrete walks lit by ornate iron lamps, running the five blocks between the Main Street Bridge and Hyacinth Street. Strings of lights lined the walks like necklaces against the sky. During the carnival, the place became a sea of people, all laughing and chatting and jostling their way from the plywood shack where they bought boiled shrimp and corn on the cob to the air gun game beneath the bridge.

The night was warm without the slightest hint of a breeze. Sweat clung to the necks of running children, strolling adults, and even the lazy folks who did nothing more than occupy the park's benches, draining giant plastic cups of lemonade.

Rene and Cassie stood next to the Crawdaddy Shack, waiting for Lara. Rene tried to keep her mind occupied. She played with the name of the booth, mixed up the letters, and decided with some amusement that *Shawdaddy Crack* was just gross. Lara had promised to meet them at eight thirty, but it was nearing nine and there was no sign of her. Rene had already left two cell messages. When she tried to text, she got an "away" prompt. Cassie was getting restless, fidgeting with the hem of her skirt and checking her nails.

A cloud of steam from the shack rolled over them and Cassie threw her hands up. "That's it. It's bad enough Lara doesn't have the common decency to call us, but I refuse to smell like a boiled mud bug for the rest of the night."

"You're right," Rene agreed. "Let's make a lap or two."

They left the shadow of the booth and stepped into the parade of people on the walk. Though it was only Friday night, the carnival was packed, and moving through the crowds was difficult. A big man with a beard running halfway down his chest bumped into Rene, nearly sending her to the concrete. He called

"'Scuse me" over his shoulder and vanished in the tide of people.

"Charming," Cassie called after the guy. She grabbed Rene by the shoulder and stabilized her. "Lame-ass ox."

"Do you see anyone from school?" Rene asked.

"Nah," Cassie said. "Eric told me everyone's down by the bridge. A bunch of seniors are hanging by the haunted house until nine, and then they're doing the carnival until it gets dusty. After that, everyone's red carpeting Frank's."

"Maybe Lara's there," Rene said.

"And maybe she's out doing crystal with Hunter Wallace."

"Lara's not that stupid."

"Of course she is," Cassie said with a laugh. "Honey, Lara's about as stupid as they come these days. And I'm over it."

"She's our friend."

"Check your definition. Friends don't blow you off. They don't lie to you."

"Lie?"

"What time did she tell you she got in the other night? You know, when her parents grounded her?"

"Midnight."

"That's crap," Cassie said angrily. She looked around the crowd. No one seemed to care what she was saying, so she kept saying it. "Little miss boy crazy didn't get in until after three."

"Three?" Rene exclaimed.

"Mm-hmm."

Rene didn't know what to say.

"And," Cassie said, "she made a scene with her mama when she came in."

"How do you know all of this?"

"Her mama called mine. Now I'm not supposed to hang with Lara anymore. And quite frankly, I see no reason to get myself in trouble if she's going to be acting all trailer trash. We have enough girls in school like that. They aren't on my A-list, so I see no reason for Lara to be on it either."

"God, I don't believe this. We have to do something."

"Well, here's your chance."

Rene followed Cassie's gaze and found Lara across the lawn, leaning against a light pole, laughing hysterically. Hunter Wallace stood next to her, smirking through his thin beard. His tattooed forearms were crossed over a Shadows Fall concert T-shirt, and a cigarette burned between two fingers. Lump Hawthorne was at Hunter's side with his arm around Tara Mae Holloway, who was six months pregnant with Lump's baby. Lump screwed the cap onto a large metal flask and handed it to Tara Mae, who lunged for the container.

And Ricky Langham, looking like a yuppie who'd gotten lost and ended up at a redneck party, completed the group. He was almost handsome, except his features were too sharp and his eyes were too cold. The Bluetooth earpiece for his cell phone rested against his head as always, making him look even more mechanical, like an android created to impersonate a teenager. The five stood in the bath of light from the tall lamp, looking like a Department of Education poster warning teens away from just about everything.

"What does she think she's doing?" Rene whispered, watching Lara grasp the lamppost tightly and spin low like a stripper about to kick her show into overdrive.

"She thinks she's having fun," Cassie replied. "And I think we'd best leave her to it."

"She's trashed."

"Fully loaded," Cassie agreed. "Which is an excellent reason to be very far away from here."

"Cassie. God, she's our friend. We can't just leave her."

"Can and will," Cassie said. "If you want to answer her cry for help, be my guest, but I highly suggest you leave it alone until she's de-iced and can think straight."

Hunter noticed Rene staring and took a drag from his cigarette. He released the smoke and let it ooze from his lips in a thick cloud that hung over his mouth and nose. A moment later his tongue shot out and flicked up and down to disperse the smoke. He chuckled and put the cigarette between his lips before grabbing Lara around the waist and pulling her close.

Disgusting, Rene thought.

"Charming," Cassie said, grasping Rene's arm. "Come on. Let's go see what the civilized people are doing. We'll leave these lovely folks to their monster truck pulls and some romantic inbreeding."

Rene took Cassie's hand off of her arm gently and pulled away. "I'll catch up in a minute."

"Do not go over there," Cassie warned.

"I'm just going to make sure Lara's okay."

"Rene, honey. You cannot fix this. Not tonight."

Rene smiled to put Cassie at ease and stepped onto the grass. "I wouldn't even try. I'm just going to talk to her for a second. You go ahead. I'll meet you at the bridge."

Despite the happy face she gave Cassie, Rene was terrified of walking up to Hunter's gang. The grass squashed under her feet, but instead of feeling soft and comforting, it felt as if it might give way any second and suck her deep into the ground. The noise at her back no longer filled her with excitement, but rather seemed like the perfect cover for her screams. Hunter saw her coming first, and he slapped Lump Hawthorne's shoulder. Lump looked up, seeming a bit dazed, but once he saw Rene coming, his eyes cleared and grew soft.

Lump had had a crush on Rene in the eighth grade. At the time, she had thought the thick-necked boy was sweet, if a little rough around the edges. He'd tried so hard to impress her back then, she'd almost felt bad for him. He'd even asked her to a movie once but was so nervous, he mumbled, "Never mind," and ran away before Rene could answer.

As for Lara, she swung on the pole again and whipped herself back into Hunter's grasp. She saw Rene on the grass and her eyes grew wide.

"Girrrrl . . . FRIEND!" she shouted.

Rene's cheeks burned red with embarrassment for Lara. Hunter just laughed and Lump scratched his head with one hand while drawing Tara Mae to his chest with the other. Tara Mae eyed Rene suspiciously, perhaps knowing about Lump's long-ago crush, perhaps just jealous of a girl who wasn't going to spend the next two decades raising a child.

Lara let go of the lamp and raced forward in a stumbling, lopsided run, reminding Rene of the Scarecrow from *The Wizard of Oz*. She had to admit, Lara could use a brain about now.

"Rene," Lara said too loudly. "Oh God. Oh God. I'm, like, so glad you're here."

Rene held Lara by the shoulders to keep her from collapsing on the grass. She tried to keep the smile pasted on her face so Lara wouldn't freak.

"How's it going?" Rene asked.

"Oh God. So much fun. So fun." Lara cackled crazily and swung out her arms. "Isn't the carnival great?"

"Yeah," Rene lied. "Let's take a walk. We'll find Cassie and get some drinks."

She had to get Lara away from Hunter.

"Totally!" Lara shouted. "Totally. Let's get Cassie." She stumbled forward, pulling Rene off balance. When she righted herself, she gripped Rene's shoulder with both hands and spluttered laughter in her ear. "Oh. Oh wait. We have to wait for Hunter and the guys."

"We'll be back," Rene said, urging Lara forward. "We'll just get Cassie."

"No," her friend said, stopping dead in her tracks. "We have to get Hunter." Lara started laughing again. "He's my man." Then, thinking she was whispering but still talking way too loud, she said, "He's huge. My God. So huge. Come on. I'll show you."

That was all Rene could take. Her cool snapped and she spun on Lara, grabbing her shoulders and shaking her. "Stop it," she said. "Just stop! Do you have any idea how much of an ass you're being?"

"What?" Lara was totally surprised. "I'm just having fun."

"You call this fun?"

Lara's eyes sparkled as if her thoughts were bits of light passing over them. Then, in a split second, the lights went out. Her jaw clenched tightly, and her brow furrowed. She yanked herself out of Rene's grasp. "I should have known you'd start this crap. God. Hunter was so right about you."

"I don't care what that loser thinks," Rene said. "You're hurting yourself and I'm not going to just sit back and watch it."

"Sure you are," Hunter said. He stepped between the two girls and glared down at Rene like she was an insect he wanted to crush. Behind his beard, Hunter's mouth was fixed in a threatening sneer. "I'm the ring-master of this *loser* circus. Your friend here is the main attraction, so kick back and enjoy the show. Or move your ass on. Otherwise you might just get fed to the lions."

"Leave her alone," Rene said, trying to step around Hunter to reach Lara. But Hunter moved quickly, sliding to the side and blocking Rene's progress.

"Seems to me you're the one in trouble here. Not her."

Rene felt a sting of panic. She faltered and stepped back.

"You call me a loser?" Hunter asked, shoving a hand deep in the pocket of his jeans. "I don't think you have a clue exactly how much there is to lose in this world.

Maybe your mama and daddy would like me to stop by for supper one night."

As he spoke, Hunter withdrew the handle of a gun. The sight of the weapon unnerved Rene further.

"Now, why don't you be a good little thing and haul your ass back to the kiddie park? Because if you stay here, you are in for some serious hurt."

"Yeah," Lara barked. She sounded like her mouth was full of rocks when she spoke. "You belong at the kiddie park. Everything is nice and safe and boring. Go play on the merry-go-round, little girl. You can't handle the real world. You can't handle anything. You just want everything to stay the same. You don't want anyone to grow up because you're so damn scared to grow up yourself."

Needles of fear worked in her chest. Rene stepped back out of Hunter's shadow. She looked at Ricky Langham, who watched the scene with a blank face, one hand on his earpiece as if he were trying to hear an important call. Tara Mae Holloway grinned as she pushed into Lump's side and wrapped an arm around his body. Lump dropped his eyes, looked at the lawn as if ashamed. Lara glared at her. It was the most hateful look Rene had ever seen, and it drove the needles deeper into her body.

We were friends, she thought.

Turning away, Rene tried to keep her cool. Tried to

keep from crying. She wouldn't run. No. Hunter would like that. He'd groove on the idea she was fleeing in terror. She felt him behind her. Hatred rolled off him in waves; it crashed over her shoulders and pushed her across the lawn, toward the carnival—toward all of the noisy people having so much fun.

Cassie and the other kids weren't under the bridge when Rene arrived. She stepped beneath its shadow and looked around. A long line had formed in front of the House of Dread. Children and teens, tickets in hand, queued up between ragged white ropes ready to enter the giant mouth of a devil painted on the front of the building. Miranda Bocage was there, giggling and leaning on the shoulder of a tall, blond-haired man who looked ten years older than she was. He leaned in and kissed her, and once their lips parted, Miranda quickly searched the crowd with her gaze, probably hoping Eric Crawford was around to see her. But Eric wasn't there and Cassie wasn't there. Besides Miranda and her date, Rene saw families and couples, smiling and eating funnel cakes from a cart. No sign of the kids from school.

It didn't really matter, though. Her night was already ruined. She didn't even bother using her cell to call Cassie. She'd rather just go home.

Did Lara really think that Rene was afraid to grow

up? Or was she just pissed off that Rene wasn't as eager to do it?

It was the drugs, Rene told herself as she wandered back into the lights of the carnival. She felt so bad that she kept her head down. The laughter from the people seemed muffled as if coming from under water. The bells and music of the booths, even the alarms that sounded when somebody won a cheap stuffed animal, rang flat and dull. Occasionally she looked up, hoping to see Cassie or some other friendly face. But all of the people looked the same to her. Just smears of features hovering above shambling bodies, like extras in a zombie movie.

After walking nearly the length of the carnival, Rene looked up and found herself standing near the Fun Zone. It was the kiddie park. A flash of embarrassment ran through Rene, and she quickly looked around to see if Lara and her new loser friends were nearby.

Inside the park, an ancient merry-go-round with cracked mirrors spun around. The miniature horses on which kids sat were blanketed in chipped and faded paint. Children cried both in glee and in fear. Some screamed.

Go play on the merry-go-round, little girl. You can't handle the real world.

She didn't see Lara or Hunter, but she moved quickly away from the merry-go-round. A couple pushed into her shoulder, and Rene stumbled to the right, nearly knocking into a line of kids and their parents. She righted herself and was about to reenter the flow of people on the midway when she saw Mason.

He stood near the front of the line. His head and shoulders were slumped. Seeing Mason this way further soured Rene's mood. She felt the impulse to go talk to him, to find out what was wrong, but she'd exceeded her drama limit for the night. She decided to say hello, and then she was going home.

Mason got to the ticket taker just as Rene reached him. He was about to enter the petting zoo, a small maze of pens set up on the hillside between the walkway and Main Street above. It wasn't much of a zoo, from what Rene could see. There was a pony tied to a tall pole hammered into the ground. A couple of goats. But mostly it was a row of rabbit cages with the lids open. Maybe ten of them.

The ticket taker was a skinny woman with sunken eyes. She wore a candy-striped apron over black jeans and a dirty orange T-shirt. On her head, perhaps as an attempt to control her greasy black hair, was a simple red bandanna tied down like a scarf. The name sewn on the breast of her apron read Fanny.

"I don't have any tickets," Mason told the woman.

"Well, you need two tickets for the zoo," Fanny replied, sounding annoyed.

Rene watched the woman's face. Why on earth had they decided she was the right person to welcome children to the petting zoo? She'd have been better positioned in front of the House of Dread.

"I've only got this," Mason said, holding out a ten-dollar bill. "Is this enough?"

Fanny's eyes lit up like a storybook witch finding a child on her doorstep. Her eyes flashed quickly from side to side to see if she was being watched by anyone with authority. She reached for the bill.

"That should be about right," Fanny said.

Before the woman's bony fingers could touch Mason's money, Rene stepped in. "Don't even," she said, startling both Mason and Fanny. Mason's mouth dropped open as if he was about to say something, but he remained silent. Rene, on the other hand . . . "What kind of a bitch steals money from a kid?"

"Hey!" the ticket taker said.

"Rene?" Mason asked. "I want to see the zoo."

"Look, Mason," Rene said. "Tickets are seventy-five cents apiece. That's like a dollar fifty. She's scamming you."

Mason listened to her words as if she were presenting him with a complicated math problem. His eyes clouded with thought. Then his face fell, and Mason nodded his head. He shoved the ten-dollar bill into his pocket and stomped away.

"I'm sorry," Rene called after him. He didn't even slow down. She turned her attention to Fanny and said, "Such a bitch."

The ticket taker puffed out her chest and opened her mouth to express outrage, but Rene was already walking away. She wanted to make sure Mason was all right.

Crap, what a night.

Rene found him sitting on a hill, not far from the petting zoo. He had his big arms draped over his knees. His head was down as if he might be crying.

You can't protect him, Rene told herself. *Maybe you can help a little, but you can't always be there. He's going to be a victim his whole life. It isn't right. It isn't fair. But it's the way the world works.*

She took a step onto the grass toward him, wondering what she could say to make Mason feel better. Not much, she knew, but it seemed like they both could use a friend right now. The grass squished under her shoe, soft and gentle.

Then the ticket taker screamed.

The shriek sliced through all of the other carnival sounds, shrill and pained as if the woman were being burned alive. Rene checked on Mason, but he seemed too depressed to care about the noise. He sat on the hill with his head down, oblivious to the happenings around him. Rene raced back toward the scream, where a crowd of people had gathered. She pushed to get close enough to see, but was shoved back and forth. The screams kept coming.

Finally, Rene worked her way close enough to the front of the crowd so that she could see. Fanny had her hands out in front of her. Her ugly, skull-thin face was wrinkled up around a screaming mouth and bulging eyes. Parents pulled their children close, held them tightly.

"Keep it away," the woman cried. "Help me. God, help me. Keep it away."

Rene looked at the space in front of the woman, but nothing stood on the walk or the grass except the curious carnival goers. Whatever terrible thing was coming for her did so only in her mind.

In the petting zoo, the goats and the pony danced nervously. The rabbits huddled in the corners of their pens.

"Keep it away!"

A man moved out of the crowd. He had his hands up in front of him. "Calm down," he said with a cool, quiet voice. "Nobody is going to hurt you."

Fanny's last screech was so high and weak it sounded like the dying whistle of a teakettle taken from the stove. Her eyes rolled back, turned white. She gasped once and then toppled over on the grass in a dead faint.

Rene pushed back, even as the rest of the crowd

Westport Free Public Library
408 Old County Road
508-636-1100

User name: Camara, Devin
Patrick
User ID: 22042000225116

Title: Mason
Author: Pendleton, Thomas,
1965-
Item ID: 32042000836803
Date due: 10/12/2016, 23:
59

moved forward. They gasped themselves. They mumbled questions and concerns. One woman even giggled nervously. Rene worked backward out of the bustling onlookers. They could deal with the crazy thief. She'd had enough for one night. It was time to go home.

8
Shades of Black

Gene Avrett walked into Dusty Smith's house without knocking. The idiot had left the door unlocked, which worked out well, because Gene didn't want to be seen lingering on the man's porch.

After a quick glance around, he stepped into a dismal room, closed the door behind him, and then locked it. A thrash-metal song blared from the sound system. The floor was covered in litter—fast-food wrappers, old issues of *Maxim* and *Penthouse*, discarded beer and soda cans. A tattered purple sofa was backed up against a filthy wall, stained with dirt and moisture. Gene covered his nose with a hand. The place stank of yeast, sweat, and garbage. All the scents stewed in the warm moist air, creating a sickening perfume.

Disgusting, he thought.

He should have sent Hunter to handle this mess.

Normally, he would have, but Gene wasn't sure exactly what approach to take with Dusty. A simple threat wasn't likely to do any good against the meth-head. Looking around the guy's house, he saw little of value to take in repayment. Even the sound system was dirt cheap. A pawnshop wouldn't give him more than ten bucks for it. Dusty had a car, but transferring the title would require paperwork, and Gene didn't want a paper trail linking him to such scum.

He'd gone to great trouble to keep his affiliation with his employees a secret. He didn't want to see all of that effort wasted. Secrecy was important. It was imperative. Gene only conducted business with Hunter face-to-face or via Instant Message. No way to trace the communications. When they did meet, it was brief, like their meeting in the bathroom of Frank's. Gene traded off the product for payment and walked away. Hunter distributed to Dusty, Lump Hawthorne, and Ricky Langham.

It was all quite perfect. Until Dusty decided to cook up the profits.

Dumb-ass hick.

Now, someone had to step up to take responsibility.

Hunter had said something about a new girlfriend. A skank, he called her. *Is she here?* Gene wondered. *Is Dusty?*

Gene checked his gloves. Latex. Boosted from the

drugstore months ago. They made his hands appear white and ghostly.

He walked through the messy living room, thought about turning off the sound system, but then thought the noise might help. He wandered into the kitchen but only stayed a moment. The sink was filled with dirty dishes. Flies buzzed over the plates and glasses, searching for bits of filth to dine upon. Three roaches scurried over the countertop and disappeared beneath an old chrome toaster with a dented side.

Gene found Dusty in a small room off of the hall. Dusty was supermodel skinny, with sunken cheeks and long blond hair that fell away from his face. His ribs showed as if they lay beneath a thick layer of dust rather than skin and muscle. He was sprawled on the bed, wearing a pair of dirty cargo shorts and one white sock. On the sole of the sock, dark patches of dirt, the shape of his foot, were ground into the fabric. Small squares of aluminum foil with dark charred circles at their centers, checkered the mattress around him. And lying on top of a pile of discarded sheets was a wooden baseball bat with someone's signature burned into the tapered handle. Gene let his gaze linger on the bat. It was the only thing in the room that didn't seem broken, stained, or rotten.

Hunter was right. Dusty'd gone on a bender. It

wasn't the first time, Gene knew. What made this particular lapse in judgment so heinous was the volume of product at stake. Dusty's last order had been ample. Was any of it left?

And now Dusty was crashed, sleeping off God knows how many days of wired wakefulness. He could be unconscious for days.

Gene wasn't that patient. He kicked the bottom of Dusty's foot hard. "Hey," he said.

Dusty didn't move.

Gene pulled the 9 mm Beretta out of his pocket, aimed the gun at Dusty's face, and worked it through the air, just tracing over the unconscious man's eyebrows and nose with its muzzle.

"Bang," Gene whispered, before returning the gun to his pocket.

He slapped Dusty's cheek. Then he slapped it again. Dusty's eyes opened and then closed. Gene cocked his arm and delivered a cracking backhanded slap to his face, and that woke Dusty up.

"Wha . . . ?"

"Oh good," Gene said, his voice twinkling with false good nature. "You're awake."

"Hey, dude," Dusty said, his eyes glazed and darting from side to side. "Why you treating me like a bitch?" Dusty rubbed the sleep from his eyes. Scratched his head, sending the long blond locks into his face. "Not cool, dude. Damn. Not cool."

Gene kept on smiling, even as his rage simmered in his throat. His whole body fed off the fury. His fingers tingled. His head grew light.

"I understand you're short this week," Gene said, stepping away from the bed. He placed his hand against the fabric of his pants, felt the gun there. His gaze came to rest on the baseball bat, nestled in the pile of sheets.

"No way," Dusty said. "I'm just going to be a little late."

"How late?"

"I don't know. A week. Two. It's *so* not a big deal."

"As I hear it, you have a new friend. A certain young lady. Word is, the two of you have gone through a significant amount of product."

"Whatever," Dusty said. "I don't know who's saying what, but they're jerking you around."

Gene looked for answers in Dusty's eyes. They didn't stop moving. They danced; they flitted like hummingbirds. He saw fear there. And while he certainly liked seeing the fear, the extent of it showed the scum was lying.

"Where is your lady friend?" Gene asked.

"She bailed. Her parents dragged her off to Metairie to visit Granny."

Gene nodded. "And when will she be back?"

"I don't know, dude," Dusty said. "Sometime next week. Why? What difference does it make?"

"I thought she might be able to confirm your story."

Dusty's face twisted into a mask of annoyance. "Dude, get out of my face. All of your weird ass mob-boss crap doesn't fly here. I brought you into this. I made you a butt load of money. So just step off. You'll get paid when I have it."

Gene's smile broadened. He pulled the gun from his pocket and gazed down the barrel at Dusty. The loser recoiled on the bed, rolled away. Dusty clutched the wall as if he could pull it down over himself for protection.

"Let's try this again," Gene said, sounding very pleased. "Are you listening?"

"Y-yes," Dusty muttered.

"You stole from me. That is unacceptable." Gene leaned over the bed. "Are you listening?"

"Y-yes," Dusty repeated. "Dude . . . Gene, just put the gun away, man. We'll totally work this out."

"You've shown me an immense amount of disrespect, and that too is unacceptable." Gene glared down at Dusty's trembling form. "Are you listening?"

"What? C'mon, man. Yeah. I'm listening. I hear you. I screwed up. I'll totally fix this. Just chill, man. Put the gun away."

Dusty was scratching at the wall now, trying to dig

through it. One of his nails snapped back. His eyes continued to flit about, looking for escape, for rescue.

"Someone has to step up," Gene said. "Someone has to take responsibility. Are you listening, Dusty?"

"God damn it, yes," Dusty cried. His voice cracked. His wild eyes filled with tears. "I'm listening, Gene. I'm listening."

"Good," Gene said.

And squeezed the trigger.

Dusty gasped. But there was no explosion. Not even a pop.

"You idiot," Gene said with a chuckle, knowing he'd left the safety on. He put the gun back in his pants. "If I shot you, the cops would be here in five minutes. You've got neighbors on both sides, and that's a powerful gun there. They'd be jabbing 911 before I got the smile off my face."

Dusty's body went limp. "Shit, man," he mumbled. "Damn."

"You've seen too many movies," Gene said, still laughing. He bent low and wrapped his hand around the baseball bat. "All that *Scarface* crap. Only a fool would try to get away with something that brash." He righted himself, grasping the bat tightly in both hands.

Dusty's eyes grew wide, seeing the club.

"And I'm no fool," Gene whispered.

Then he started swinging.

Rene walked with Mason. They had left the carnival behind and wandered through the nice neighborhood on the river's edge, but now they were passing into the Ditch. There were fewer streetlamps here. Lights burned behind closed blinds in the smaller homes set close to the street, but their glow didn't even reach the sidewalk. During the day the Ditch wasn't so bad. It was just another neighborhood, and yeah, the folks didn't have as much money, but it wasn't a total low-rent hood. She felt safe enough walking with Mason, but wondered how safe she'd feel once she left him at his door.

Still, he'd looked so miserable at the carnival. After leaving the scene by the petting zoo, Rene had walked back to where he was sitting and asked if he was ready to go home.

"S'pose," he'd said.

Rene tried to get him to talk during their walk, but Mason was withdrawn. His mouth was set in a frown, and his shoulders slumped.

They crossed onto Pecan Street. Mason's house was still five blocks away. Feeling uncomfortable in the silence, Rene tried to start a new conversation.

"I wonder what happened to the petting zoo lady," Rene said. "She just freaked out. It was so weird."

"When I was little, my best friend was Lightning,"

Mason said, surprising Rene by changing the subject. "Lightning was fun and he liked hamburgers and chasing his ball."

"I remember," Rene said. Lightning had been a beautiful golden retriever that always seemed to be smiling. Mason and that dog were inseparable for nearly six months, but then Lightning ran away. Or at least, that's what Mason's aunt Molly said. Rene couldn't imagine the animal just running off, not when he seemed to love Mason so much. "He was a good dog."

"And he went away," Mason added. "He never came home, and Aunt Molly wouldn't let me have another dog. I guess she blamed me for him running away. I really missed him. A long time later, I came home from school and went up to my room and there *was* another dog. It was lying on my bed. It didn't move. But it wasn't like Lightning. It scared me bad. It looked like a monster from a movie. Its fur was all dirty and torn out in places and its body was all thin and had bugs crawling on it. One of its eyes hung out all funny."

Rene's throat knotted up. "Mason, that's awful. Why are you telling me this?"

"That's what the lady saw," he whispered. "She saw that dog, only it wasn't just lying down."

Rene looked at Mason, but his face hadn't changed. His mouth was still drooping in a frown. She thought about what he'd just said and it creeped her out, because he didn't say, "I think that's what the lady saw," or "I bet that's what the lady saw." He just stated it outright, as if he could know what terrible thing that nasty woman's mind had created.

"It was probably drugs," Rene said. That made her think of Lara, and she shook off a sudden chill.

"S'pose."

"Well, I think she had it coming," Rene added, hoping it would make Mason feel better, though she knew it was a terrible thing to say.

"Someone's got to step up," Mason replied.

"What?"

"Nothing."

"Mason, are you okay?" Rene asked. "For the last few days you've seemed really down."

"I don't want to be a doorknob."

"I don't understand."

"Gene says I'm dumb as a doorknob, and I don't want to be."

Rene reached out and touched Mason's arm. "You're not dumb. He's just being mean to you."

"I *am* dumb. And I'm always gonna be, and I don't wanna be."

He sounded angry now, and Rene didn't want to upset him any more. Besides, she was struck by the strangest thought, which came to her out of nowhere: *He wants to grow up and I don't. But neither of us has a choice. He will always be innocent, and I have to leave that behind.*

"You're not dumb," Rene said again.

She couldn't help but think Mason's aunt never should have let him go to school, at least not to Marchand High. There he had to witness other kids becoming adults when he would never be able to do it himself. Of course his home life wasn't much better, or so Rene supposed. His aunt was hardly ever around, and his brother . . . well, his brother was just wicked. If Gene had anything to do with Mason, Rene imagined it wasn't good.

A disturbing thought occurred to her then.

Gene put that dog in Mason's room. He dug up some buried stray and left it on his brother's bed to scare him. Or worse. Maybe it wasn't a stray. What if that rotten dog was actually Lightning? What if Gene . . .

Oh, that's too sick.

Even Gene wouldn't . . .

Oh God, he would.

"Why don't we get some ice cream tomorrow?" Rene said. "My treat. We'll go to Frank's and get a couple of double scoops."

This perked Mason up. In fact, it seemed as if a switch in his brain was thrown, and he went from miserable to happy in just under two seconds. He stopped walking and turned to her with sparkling eyes and a grin on his lips.

"Strawberry?" Mason asked.

"I think that can be arranged."

Gene Avrett stood in the hallway of Dusty Smith's house. He looked back into the room. He saw the blood and Dusty's crumpled body. He saw the stained baseball bat lying where he'd discarded it on the bed.

Dusty was dead.

The knowledge that he'd killed sparked and crackled through Gene's nerves like he'd just won the lottery. It was thrilling. Since the night he had tried to suffocate Mason, Gene had wanted to know what murder felt like. He knew well enough what killing birds and squirrels was like, and it was okay. But people? Now he had his answer.

You killed him. You're a murderer. If the cops come down on you for this, it won't be a handful of years for a drug charge. They won't care if he was a low-rent hick or not. You're eighteen. You'll be tried as an adult. No way around that.

But I didn't mean to do it.

But you did. You knew this was going to happen from the moment you slid on those gloves. Why else would you have put them on? Germ phobia? I don't think so. Premeditated.

81

That's what they'll say. And every damn thing you've ever worked for will be gone. Blown away with Dusty's last breath.

Are you listening, Gene? Are you listening?

"Burn it down," he whispered to himself. A fire would destroy any evidence. They'd think Dusty just got too high while sparking another foil.

But what about his broken skull? Unless the roof comes down in exactly the right way, they'll know he was killed before the blaze and someone else started the fire. Besides, the place would be swarming with firemen in five minutes. The police would be right behind them.

"So, hide the body. Hide the bat. Scrub the place down. Make it look like Dusty hit the road."

Don't be an idiot. You'd never get the place clean enough. They have those blood lights that show spatter marks no matter how well you clean. And you didn't bring your car. What are you going to do, carry him on your shoulder?

"Just leave," he muttered. "No one knows Dusty was working for you." No one except Hunter. More than likely, Hunter would be the prime suspect, and he's tight with an alibi. He's at the carnival.

Gene waited for his mind to counter this solution with some fresh bit of logic, but his mind only hummed. It must be the right answer.

"Good," he said. Once the word left his lips, a rain of

confidence fell through him.

Gene left the hallway and walked into the bathroom. He turned on the light and checked himself in the mirror. His shirt had a few small drops of blood on it. Hardly noticeable. He searched his face and neck but found them clean. Gene looked at the gloves. They were a mess. Small trickles of crimson veined the ghostly pale latex. He would take them off outside and burn them when he got home. He'd burn all of his clothes. Even the shoes.

Footprints?

Gene hurried back to the bedroom and eased his way inside, checked the floor for any telltale marks. But he'd gotten lucky. Very lucky.

"Am I *supposed* to get away with this?" he wondered aloud.

He spent another five minutes in the house, thinking and looking. He tried to remember every cop show he'd ever seen to make sure he left no clues for the authorities. It would be days before anyone noticed a punk like Dusty was missing. It could be weeks before anyone found the body.

Just a bad drug deal, the police would think. They probably wouldn't spend more than a week checking into it.

Gene walked through Dusty's living room. He

carefully turned off the sound system and the overhead light. A lamp still burned in the corner. He'd leave that on so the place looked inhabited.

At the door, he did a final mental check and considered himself free and clear. The thrill of swinging the bat returned to him in a high electric wave.

The back door, his mind told him. *Go out the back. Slip through the yards.*

"Yes. Excellent."

But when Gene reached the back door and the window beside it, he saw the error of this plan. No fences separated Dusty's house from his neighbors'. A group of rednecks in trucker caps and jeans were having a cookout in the backyard of one of the houses. Gene looked at them angrily as if they'd planned their party to ruin his night. They were probably the only people in town who hadn't gone to the carnival. Bastards. The minute Gene opened the door, all heads would turn his direction. It would look suspicious, even to those Neanderthals.

Gene returned to the front of the house. He took a deep breath and opened the door. He walked out onto the porch casually as if just leaving from a friendly visit. He even waved at the opening as if saying goodbye before pulling the door closed behind him.

Perfect. Just visiting.

He turned to the street and stopped.

There, on the sidewalk, in front of the house on his left, was Rene Denton, his retard brother's little friend. She was walking alone and had barely paused, but she'd looked at the house. Had she seen him? Were the shadows of the porch enough to shield his identity?

Gene didn't know. But he wasn't going to take any chances.

9
Still Life

Rene Denton was uneasy because she was embarrassed. Yesterday she'd invited Mason out for ice cream to make him feel better, and she'd kept her word, but now, sitting across the table from him at Frank's Grill, she hoped no one from school saw her. Especially Cassie.

And of course she felt bad for thinking such a thing.

Frank's was busy as usual. Strangers—folks from other parishes who were in town for the carnival—occupied most of the chrome stools and the booths with their red vinyl upholstery.

"This is really good," Mason said, driving his spoon into the mushy ice cream.

"I'm glad you like it."

"Thank you."

"You're welcome," Rene said. She noticed a fat glob

of strawberry ice cream on the corner of his mouth. She reached out with her napkin and wiped it away.

Mason's cheeks turned bright red. He pulled back and scrubbed his face dramatically with his own napkin.

"I think I got it."

"Thank you," he repeated.

"Are you going back to the carnival tonight?" Rene asked. "Maybe Molly will take you out."

Mason looked worried. He shook his head and shoveled more ice cream into his mouth.

"I'll bet that nasty woman won't be there tonight. Then you could pet the animals."

Mason kept shaking his head. He swallowed his ice cream and put the spoon down. "Aunt Molly is making fried chicken, and she rented a movie for me. And she said it was a special night, so I have to be home for dinner. Dinner and a movie, she said. Her fried chicken isn't as good as Mama's, but it's good."

"Do you remember your mother?"

"S'pose."

"I bet you miss her," Rene said.

"She went away," Mason said sadly. "Everyone goes away. Gene told me so. Like Mama and Daddy and Lightning. One day Aunt Molly will go away too. And Gene. But that'll be okay, I think. I think it'll be okay if Gene goes away."

He looked at her with concern, as if he thought

he'd just said something really terrible and expected Rene to be angry with him.

"I think so too," she said. "I think Gene going away would be just fine."

"I shouldn't-a said that. He's family. Family's all you got."

"He's mean to you though, isn't he?"

"I never learn," Mason mumbled, dropping his head. "Dumb as a doorknob."

"No you're not," Rene said. She reached across the table and touched his arm. "He has no right to say that to you. None. He's just doing it to be mean."

"Gene wouldn't do that."

"Mason, I know he's your brother . . ."

"Family's all you got."

". . . but you can't let him bully you like that. Okay? When he's doing that, you have to tell him to stop, or you have to leave the room. He has no right to call you dumb or to hurt you. None. If he does, you stand up to him and you tell him to stop it."

Easier said than done, Rene knew. Gene wasn't some lame high-school bully. Damn that aunt of his for not doing anything. She had to know what was going on under her own roof. How could she not stop Gene's cruelty, unless she was as afraid of the boy as everyone else was?

They sat quietly for a bit. Rene kept her eyes on Mason. He looked confused and uncomfortable. He fidgeted with his napkin and shot quick glances out the window.

"I don't like being by myself," he said quickly. "Gene says that if I don't learn, I'm going to be all alone, and I don't want to be all alone. It's like being in a box with no light. It's scary. No one to talk to or play with." He lowered his head and plopped the spoon in his bowl. "I wish the ice cream wasn't melted."

Rene laughed a bit and covered her mouth with a hand. Mason's sudden subject change took her off guard. There he was, talking about his fear of being alone, and then he laments something so simple as a scoop of melting ice cream.

She lifted her coffee cup for a sip and then paused. A dull ache rose in her belly when she realized he hadn't changed the subject at all. People leaving. Ice cream liquefying. It was all the same to him. She put down her coffee mug.

"You won't be alone," Rene said. "One of these days, you're going to have a lot of friends. And you'll always have me."

"S'pose."

"Mason, you will."

And though she suspected it was a lie, it seemed to

cheer him. Mason dipped his head—a quick nod—and a small smile touched the edges of his mouth. She continued, "And Frank's Grill will always have strawberry ice cream, so I think you're going to be just fine."

"It's good," Mason said, looking into his dish with its pool of pink liquid.

"Yes, it is," Rene replied.

Three hours later, Gene stood at the urinal in the bathroom at Frank's. Hunter stood next to him, tapping on the wall.

"We have a problem." Gene looked at his hands, felt certain he saw blood there, just between his thumb and index finger. He scrubbed the place with his fingers.

"Yeah? What problem?"

"You know Rene Denton? Lives out on Hyacinth?"

"Yeah. Total bitch. I'm slammin' her best friend." Hunter Wallace laughed.

"Interesting."

"What's the problem?"

"She's seen something that I'd like for her not to have seen."

"You want me to put a scare into her?"

"I'm thinking of something a little more definitive."

"What the hell does that mean?"

"This isn't a vocabulary lesson. Just take care of it."

"Cool."

"Indeed. Cool."

"You figure out what to do about Dusty yet?" Hunter asked.

"I have some ideas," Gene replied, rubbing at the tender skin on his hand.

10
iconography

The carnival carried on in Riverfront Park through that warm autumn afternoon. Farmers and ranchers and families from the city descended on the town and mingled with the residents. As night fell, the noise and excitement of the midway grew.

The body of Dusty Smith still lay on the rumpled bloody sheets in a house at the center of the Ditch. His phone rang every hour or so—customers looking for a bit of the drug he used to provide them.

Only three blocks away in his bedroom, Mason Avrett looked at a series of pictures he'd drawn over the last two weeks—since the last time Gene visited his room and forced him to step up and take responsibility. In those days, his hand had scribbled one nightmare after another on the clean sketch-pad sheets.

A dog shrunken and disfigured in death, with dirty matted

fur and one eye dangling from a socket . . .

A flock of gruesome birds with tattered black wings and chipped beaks . . .

A monster that looked like his brother Gene, only with long, apelike arms ending in knobby, blunt clubs . . .

Other terrible things appeared on those pages, but these were the repeating images.

Now, with his aunt's fried chicken warming his tummy, he couldn't understand why he'd drawn them or what they meant. Mason thought the pictures were ugly. They weren't nice. So he stacked up the pages and put them in a drawer under a pile of shirts. When he returned to his bed, he thought about his fun afternoon with Rene. The ice cream was really good, and what Rene said had made him feel better, just like when his mama used to hold him and give him a cookie when Gene did mean things.

Maybe Gene wasn't trying to help him. Even though they were family, and family was all you got, maybe Gene was just hateful and bad.

And Rene Denton sat in a movie theater with Cassie Ferguson, who was telling her all about Eric Crawford, who'd actually asked for her digits last night when they ran into each other at the carnival. Cassie played it cool and said she might go out with him if he called, but Rene *knew* she would. There was no question.

Then you'll be busy all the time and I'll have to make new friends, Rene thought. *Or be alone*.

And beneath the arching arms of a willow tree near the river, away from the carnival that roared only a few dozen yards away, Lara stood in the shadows with Hunter Wallace, Ricky Langham, Lump Hawthorne, and his girlfriend, Tara Mae. Lara did a bump of crystal off the back of Hunter's hand, snorting the drug deep into her sinuses. She flipped her hair back and wiped at her nose, enjoying the burning sensation against the delicate membranes in her head.

Hunter smiled and nodded, handing a flask to her.

"Awesome," Lara said, upending the metal container and washing the back of her throat with a shot of Wild Turkey.

The three other kids looked at them. Ricky wore his earpiece and had a blank, robotic look on his face as he always did, but Lump looked nervous. Tara Mae, who kept rubbing her rounded belly absently, just looked drunk.

This blows, Lara thought. She wanted to laugh and party.

"What's up?" she asked. "You all look like we're going to a funeral."

The comment brought a crooked grin to Ricky's face and Tara barked three short, high-pitched giggles. Lump just looked at his shoes.

Hunter took Lara's arm lightly and turned her away

from the others. He led her out from under the willow tree to a patch of grass near the river's edge. Behind him the carnival lights looked blurry, like chalk dots smeared by careless fingers.

"You're going to do something for me," Hunter said.

"Don't I do everything for you?" Lara said with a giggle to make the question sound dirty.

"Yeah, whatever," Hunter replied. "It's about that friend of yours. Rene."

"God, don't even talk about her," Lara said, her system thrumming now with the bump of crystal. "She's such a bitch."

"She is," Hunter said. "We need to teach her a lesson, right?"

Lara tried to process her boyfriend's words, but they got tangled in the Wild Turkey and meth. She didn't understand. "You're not going to hurt her, are you?"

"Do you care?"

"No," Lara said. She laughed too loudly, feeling a strange mix of excitement and fear. Even though she was wasted and trying to impress her boyfriend, Lara wasn't sure. Part of her remembered what a good friend Rene was.

Yeah, she used to be cool. Now she's all like a parent or a cop or something.

"Look, we just want to punk her for disrespecting us," Hunter explained.

"Oh totally," Lara said. "We could egg her house or leave dog crap on the stoop."

"Yeah, right. Like that. Only I had something a little more creative in mind. Are you in?"

"Totally!"

"Cool. Here's what you're going to do."

11
Focal Point

Rene and Cassie walked over the red carpet. The scents of popcorn and nacho cheese sauce filled the air. The movie, a typical teen comedy, was over, and now the audience wandered toward the glass doors, passing the people waiting in line for the next show. Both girls pulled cell phones from their shoulder bags and turned them on. Rene noticed she had missed a call. Cassie looked at her display screen and apparently saw no message alerts, because she said, "Figures," and tossed the phone back into her bag.

"Eric didn't call?" Rene asked, already knowing the answer.

"No-*ooo*," Cassie said, adding an extra syllable to express her frustration.

"He will. He's just playing that stupid boy game. He probably has a three-day rule."

"Who teaches them this crap?" Cassie wanted to know.

Rene pointed over her shoulder with a thumb. "We just sat through ninety minutes of it."

Outside in the warm night air, people stood on the sidewalk, many of them chatting. Cassie looked annoyed, her pretty face scrunched up with thought. She twirled a lock of hair around a finger.

"So what do we do now?" Cassie asked. "It's only, like, nine o'clock."

"You drove," Rene reminded her. "Where do you want to go?"

They tried to think of someplace new, but the conversation always came back to Frank's.

"Just don't let me order fries," Cassie said as she opened the car door. "I cannot deal with carbs this week."

The restaurant was busier than it had been that afternoon when Rene and Mason stopped in for ice cream. People were shoved into booths or standing in crowds around the counter, but the girls still managed to get a table. Cassie immediately brightened up. Rene watched her friend continually search the room with darting glances.

She was totally scanning for Eric. It made Rene a

little jealous. She hadn't had a boy to look for since Carter Dane.

The school year is just starting, she told herself as she sat in the booth. *There's plenty of time to meet someone. I've got plenty of time.*

"This is awesome," Cassie said. Her eyes brightened and she waved frantically.

Rene turned, the vinyl screeching under her backside as she looked in the direction of Cassie's wave. Four kids from school, three football players and a girl named Connie, stood at the end of the counter. Connie waved back happily. The football players all nodded their heads. At the table in front of this gang, Miranda Bocage sat with the older guy from the night before. She looked furious, stabbing her diet cola with her straw as the man spoke to her.

"And it's early yet," Cassie continued. "By ten, this place will be slammin'."

Yeah, Rene thought, *and by eleven, we'll all be up at the Hollow lighting a fire and drinking beers.*

The outdoor parties at the Hollow happened every few weeks. Sometimes they were planned with invitations circulated on the internet or handed out in the school's halls. Other times, they just happened. Either way, they were a lot of fun, unless Hunter and his thugs showed up to tease and bully everyone.

Her thoughts began drifting back to Lara, but Rene didn't want to deal with any of that right now. She ordered coffee from the waitress and waited for Cassie to order her french fries, which she always did, even when Rene reminded her about the carbs. Rene decided to enjoy the festivities in the restaurant. Lara would have to take care of herself.

Rene's cell phone rang and she snagged it out of her bag on the second ring.

"Hello?"

"Rene," Lara said. Her voice was low and nervous. It sounded as if Lara wasn't willing to be forgotten just yet. "Are you there?"

"Yes," Rene said, half wishing she'd ignored the call.

"I really need to talk to you. It's totally important."

"So talk."

Rene heard fragments of words, but the noisy crowd made it hard to make out what Lara was saying. Across the table, Cassie looked around, smiling. Suddenly her eyes lit up and her cheeks flared red, and then she lowered her head to stare at the table. Rene turned and saw Eric Crawford with some of his buddies approaching the table. Lara kept talking, but Rene couldn't make out a word of it.

"Hold on," Rene said. "I have to go outside." She covered the mouthpiece and told Cassie she'd see her in a minute. Then she scooted out of the booth.

"You can't leave me!" Cassie said anxiously.

"You're a big girl," Rene said, "and I'll be right back."

Rene said hi to Eric and Orin Unger as she made her way down the aisle. Outside, she turned left and walked several feet from the door.

"Now, what's going on?" Rene asked.

"Can you meet me?" Lara asked.

"After last night? I don't think so."

"Please, Rene. I'm scared. Really scared. I'm sorry about last night. So sorry, but I need to see you. It's Hunter. . . . He . . . God, I can't even say it."

A list of terrible things Hunter might have done unfolded in Rene's mind. She pictured the tattooed thug in her mind, imagined him hitting Lara, saw him pull his gun from his pants. What had he done?

"Where are you?"

"I don't know," Lara said, panicked. "I ran out of his house. I'm in the woods somewhere. You have to come get me."

"The woods? Where?"

"By his house! God, I don't know."

Rene thought about Hunter's neighborhood. It was on the opposite side of town from the Ditch—not that his family was living large. Hunter's mother had inherited the house from her parents. It was in a nice neighborhood, but the place was run-down, with two old muscle cars up on blocks in the side yard.

"Oh," Lara said quickly. "I think I'm near the Hollow. Can you meet me at the Hollow? Please?"

Seeing a chance to finally talk some sense into her friend, Rene agreed. "I can meet you. Cassie and I are at Frank's, so it will take us a while to get there."

"You can't bring Cassie," Lara said quickly. "Please? The last thing I need is her acting like Miss Southern Perfection right now. I just need to talk to you. Please?"

"Okay. I'll be there. Just calm down."

"Hurry," Lara said.

"I will."

Rene walked along the wooded stretch of road. Alone.

Eric Crawford was more than enough to keep Cassie occupied for an hour. So Rene had lied and said she had to run home for something.

Cassie had said, "I'll be here."

Rene made a right onto a dark trail that wound through the pines and dogwoods. The trees fell behind her, so tall they blocked out the sky and the stars. She stepped over a fallen branch and felt a tingling current of fear run down her spine. What had Hunter done to Lara, she wondered? Not knowing made it all the worse. Rene imagined terrible things. Had he freaked on her? Beaten her? Raped her? Rene trembled. It could have been anything. And worse, Hunter might have followed Lara into the woods. Even now he might be prowling the darkness with his gun. Sweat erupted on Rene's neck as she picked her way along the trail.

Farther down the path, she heard movement in the woods. She thought to call out for Lara, but what if it wasn't her? Rene kept walking, her eyes slowly adjusting to the gloom. Finally the tight row of trees opened up into a rounded patch of beaten-down dirt, which appeared a shade lighter than the cloying darkness surrounding it.

The Hollow was an old campground, long since deserted by families for afternoon outings. Now the area was reserved for high-school parties and burners who wanted to get wasted amid the glory of nature. Rene remembered the fire pit in the middle of the clearing and made sure to walk around it.

"Rene?" Lara whispered from across the clearing.

Rene squinted but couldn't see her friend through the darkness. She remembered an old picnic bench on the far side of the clearing, imagined that was where Lara would be, and made her way toward it.

Movement in the bushes at her back startled her. *Hunter?* Rene jumped and spun around, but the oppressive night hid whatever had made the noise. A branch snapped to her right.

"Lara?" Rene said. "Where are you?"

"Over here," her friend whispered.

Just then a flashlight beam broke the darkness. She'd been right: Lara was at the picnic bench. Though she couldn't see her friend well with the glare of light beaming out at her, Rene walked toward it, covering her eyes with one hand.

Rene didn't even think to wonder how Lara had come across a flashlight while fleeing Hunter's house.

A can crunched under her foot, and Rene leaped forward.

"Are you okay?" she asked, moving quickly toward the picnic bench.

"I'm fine," Lara said.

Rene paused. Something in her friend's voice—humor?—made her stop.

"What's going on?" Rene asked.

"This!" Lara said.

The flashlight jumped as if yanked high by a cord. Then, Rene felt something cold hit her face and hair and neck. She heard a hissing like the sound of a snake and felt long thin trails wrapping around her. Lara's giggles filled the Hollow as the flashlight's beam danced against the darkness.

Rene backed away with a yelp, and saw the long slender ropes leaping at her through the night. Only then, with her heart thundering in her chest, did Rene understand what was covering her.

Silly String?

"I don't believe this!" Rene shouted, already trying to pick the stuff from her hair. "You brought me all the way out here for some childish prank!"

"Buuuuuuurn," Lara said with a laugh. "So burned."

"What the hell is wrong with you?"

"You've been punked!" Lara yelled.

The flashlight continued its dance. But suddenly other lights came on around her.

Rene turned and saw Lump Hawthorne working his way across the Hollow toward her. She whirled around. Ricky Langham emerged from a thick bush.

Hunter! Rene thought. *Oh God. Hunter.*

She turned her back to Lara. Hunter was standing in the center of the Hollow, holding a lantern in one hand and a thick length of tree branch in the other.

"You think you're so smart," Lara said. "We totally got you."

"Yeah," Rene said, taking a step to the left. "You got me."

"Don't act all innocent, you so deserved it."

Does she even know what she's done? Rene wondered. Already tears were welling in her eyes. Hunter wouldn't go to all this trouble to play some juvenile prank on her. No way. Something worse was going to happen if she didn't get out of there, and fast. But did Lara know it?

Rene broke to the left, but before she could get

up any real speed, Lump's arm went across her chest and he pulled her into a tight hug. Rene screamed but was cut off by a slap against the side of her head. She reached up and drove her nails into Lump's arm, raking trenches in it.

"Hey," Lump growled. He slapped the side of her head again and shoved her into the center of the Hollow, only two feet from Hunter Wallace.

Hunter glared down at her, his face lit from the side by Lara's flashlight. A piece of Silly String dropped in front of Rene's eye, brushing over her lashes. Rene wiped it away with a sheen of tears.

"You played the wrong game with the wrong players," Hunter told her.

"Totally," Lara yelped. Another fit of giggles filled the Hollow. "I can't wait to tell everyone at school about the look on your face."

"Why, Lara?" Rene asked. "How could you?"

Across the clearing, Ricky Langham lifted a piece of charred wood from a long-dead fire out of the pit. In front of Rene was Hunter's evil grin.

"She's a little slow," he said.

"You can't do this. Cassie knows I came here." It was a lie, but if Hunter and the others thought Cassie was watching her back they might think twice about hurting her.

"Then Cassie is going to get a call in about twenty

minutes," Hunter replied, casually swinging his branch through the air. "Apparently, you never showed up."

Cold terror flowed down Rene's throat. It hit her stomach like a fist. Her nerves jittered frantically as she tried to calculate a path of escape. But Lump and Hunter and Ricky formed a half circle around her. On the other side were Lara and the picnic bench.

"Why are we gonna call Cassie?" Lara asked.

"Because of what they're going to do to me," Rene cried. "God, Lara. Help me!"

"She isn't going to help," Hunter said confidently.

Desperation flared in Rene and she broke to her right. Arms came out at her. She scratched and she kicked, but she wasn't able to break loose. She was a doll being tossed around by cruel children.

"Next time," Hunter said, "you mind your business."

Then, he swung the thick tree branch. It hit the side of Rene's head, cutting her scalp and sending her sideways into Lump Hawthorne. Her vision blurred. She opened her mouth to scream, but another branch crunched against the back of her head. She dropped to her knees and looked up at her tormentors pleadingly. Their names ran through her head in a rapid loop. HunterWallaceLaraPearceLumpHawthorneRickyLangham. So many Ls. *No*, she thought. *You have to think clearly. Stop this.* But she couldn't. The names kept playing over, changing and condensing like the game she played with other words. Desperation tangled her thoughts until nothing made sense. So many Ls.

wall arump am

L-L-L-L-L-L

wall arump am

Hunter Wallace grinned down at her. He tossed his flashlight to the ground and grasped the tree branch in both hands. Then he lifted it high.

"Please . . ." Rene managed to say.

Hunter slammed the branch against the top of her head.

Rene had never known such pain, and it was just beginning.

12

Figure in Repose

Cassie Ferguson followed Eric Crawford, Orin Unger, and about two dozen other kids into the woods. Too many lowbrows, in town for the carnival, were shoving their way into Frank's, and its appeal was hemorrhaging. So Eric suggested that everyone head out to the Hollow, where the party could really crank up. Cassie had tried to call Rene, but her friend wasn't answering. She even tried the home number, but Rene's mom said she hadn't come home yet. That was kind of weird. Still, the mystery only distracted her for a second or two. Before she knew it, Eric's arm, covered in his letterman's jacket, was slipping around her waist and guiding her through the woods to the old campground.

She hadn't expected the night to turn out so epically wonderful. Going to the movie with Rene was okay and Frank's was fun, but she totally didn't expect Eric to show up and offer her a ride up to the Hollow.

"Hey," Eric whispered, slowing his steps.

The other kids continued into the woods, dark shapes against a darker background. They looked like black ghosts, disappearing among the gloomy trees. Cassie shivered.

"Yeah?" she responded.

"Do you think Rene likes Orin?" Eric asked. "I mean, it's cool if she doesn't, but he thinks she's hot, so I told him I'd do some recon."

Cassie didn't know. The only boy Rene had talked about for a whole year was that Carter Dane kid who'd died in the spring. Well, him and Mason Avrett, but Cassie knew Rene didn't feel *that* way about Mason. At least she hoped not. That would be gross. Orin was cute enough, and his daddy did own the town's biggest car dealership. Why *wouldn't* Rene like him?

"She might," Cassie said with just enough mischief in her voice to suggest she did know the answer, and that the answer was yes.

"Cool," Eric said. "Miranda, like, hated all of my friends, and so, when we hung out, it was just like the two of us, and it totally sucked. Maybe they'll hook up and we can all hang out sometime."

Cassie's heart fluttered. Was he saying what she thought he was saying? Did Eric already consider her his girlfriend? They hadn't even had a real date yet. He couldn't have meant that, but the idea thrilled her.

"Sure," she said, trying to maintain control.

They were the last of the kids to enter the Hollow. Eric guided her into the clearing as Orin and one of the football players knelt over the fire pit, lighters in hand. A few small wads of paper lit up, and Orin scrambled around the pit, grabbing stray leaves from the dirt and dropping them onto the tiny blaze.

"They're going to need, like, some real wood," Eric said. He pulled a flat pint bottle of vodka out of his letterman's jacket and handed it to Cassie. "Why don't you get comfortable, and I'll, like, round some up."

"I can help," Cassie said, a little too eagerly.

"I don't want you to ruin your outfit, hauling dirty twigs and, like, branches and junk."

"I'll be okay," Cassie told him.

So they walked to the edge of the clearing. Cassie found a narrow twig and quickly snatched it from the ground. Then another and another. She followed Eric into the bushes between the thick trunks of two trees, gathering up bits of wood as she went. Behind her, the kids shouted and laughed, already in the party spirit. One of the boys poured a long trail of alcohol onto the dwindling fire and it erupted in a great gout of flame. Another boy tossed an empty beer carton on, bringing a more consistent burn, lighting up the clearing and its edges. Ahead of her, Eric paused. Startled but unable to stop, she walked right into his back.

"Oh crap," he muttered. "Oh holy crap."

"What?" Cassie asked, stepping around him.

"Don't look, Cassie."

But it was too late. Even in the gloom she saw what lay in the dirt at Eric's feet. The body's arms and legs were twisted and bent, splayed out from the torso in odd directions. She recognized the outfit. The pants, now torn. The blouse, now stained. They were the only things she could recognize. The face was swollen and cut and lay under a mask of blood.

Cassie screamed. The branches fell from her hands, and she covered her face with her palms. Eric's arms went around her, and Cassie fell into his chest, shrieking in terror.

Rene! Oh God, Rene. No.

PART
TWO

13
The Artist's Medium

Gene stared at his television. The sound was muted; he'd heard the reports all day and was getting sick of the oh-so-concerned dramatics of the anchormen and -women. So he just watched: saw the wooded area his classmates called the Hollow, saw a blowhard cop talking to reporters, saw a yearbook picture of Rene Denton flash on the screen. His blood simmered with rage.

She should be dead, he thought. *She should be dead*.

Hunter had screwed up. Rene Denton was alive because the tattooed fool couldn't be trusted with a simple chore. Gene had fumed over the idiot's incompetence all day, and since a public confrontation with Hunter would be indiscreet considering recent events, someone else had to step up.

That's what little brothers were for.

Gene waited for his aunt to go to bed before he crept

downstairs to the kitchen. He pulled two oranges from a tacky plastic fruit bowl and fed them into the neck of a white tube sock. Bouncing the sock lightly, Gene jiggled the oranges down to the toe. He thumped the weighted fabric against his thigh and liked the feel of it.

He climbed the stairs, still unable to believe the extent of Hunter's screwup. One bullet, one well-placed knife blade, and all of their troubles would have vanished like breath on glass. But no: Hunter had tried to get creative. And yes, Gene realized that he too had gone the bludgeoning route with Dusty. He'd opted for a baseball bat instead of his gun, but that was a practical decision—the *right* decision. Hunter's choice of weapon was ridiculous—a tree branch. Christ, what was he . . . a caveman? Then the imbecile didn't even finish the work.

He'd Instant Messaged Hunter earlier in the evening to find out what the hell had gone wrong. The idiot's response infuriated him:

A bunch of lame-ass kids showed up to party. We heard them coming and dragged the bitch into the woods, then got the hell out.

As if it should have been a surprise that the high-school lemmings would show up at the Hollow on a

116

Saturday night. They were *always* there Saturday nights. Hunter should have known better. He should have picked a location with real isolation.

Fool, Gene thought, bouncing the sock against his leg. *A dangerous and damned fool.*

Upstairs Gene didn't pause at Mason's door. He grabbed the knob, pushed it open and walked right in.

Then Gene Avrett froze where he stood.

He'd expected to find Mason in bed, already asleep. Gene liked to wake the "doorknob" for his punishment. Seeing the groggy, good-natured expression on the brat's face suddenly jarred awake and alive with fright always entertained him. But Mason wasn't asleep. Gene wasn't even sure he was standing in Mason's room.

His little brother's bed was there, and Mason was sitting on it, but the bed and boy were situated in the middle of a green lawn, in a bath of buttery sunlight. A dog—*Lightning?*—bounded in circles around the bed with a yellow tennis ball firmly grasped in his drooling jaws. At the foot of the bed sat Rene Denton, wearing a white dress she should have outgrown ten years ago. On the bed between Mason and Rene was a checked tablecloth with a picnic lunch laid out on it.

Gene backed up a step. He convinced himself that he was dreaming. At some point, he must have fallen asleep in his room. Going down to the kitchen for oranges, his angry walk through the house, Mason's room—all a dream.

Gene took another look at his brother. Mason sat on the bed with his eyes closed. A deep frown began to pull down the edges of the doorknob's mouth.

Suddenly Gene was less comfortable with the fantastical surroundings.

Mason's head dipped lower.

The golden retriever appeared in front of the bed. Its lips pulled back into a ferocious growl, though Gene heard no sound emerge. The dog—*Could it really be Mason's boyhood mutt?*—crouched, readying its body to spring.

Gene released a tiny groan from his throat before turning and hurrying down the hall. He reached his bedroom door and turned back to see if the dog was attacking. But it was nowhere to be seen.

At the end of the hall, Mason stood framed in his doorway. He glared down the corridor at Gene.

Is the doorknob actually angry?

Did he find out that Denton's in the hospital?

No. Molly's been shielding Mason from the news. He couldn't know.

But something's buzzing in that soft head of his.

It doesn't matter. This is just a dream.

Mason slammed the door, and Gene entered his room, wondering when he would wake up.

Pastels

Aunt Molly woke Mason on Monday morning the way she always did, quietly calling his name from the door of his bedroom. Mason yawned and stretched. Aunt Molly told him his breakfast was ready and Mason said, "'Kay." He was climbing out of bed when he remembered the mind picture of the park he'd drawn last night and the way Lightning had scared Gene.

He saw the mind picture, Mason thought. *I wonder what else I can make him see.*

Suddenly, he was terribly excited, like it was Christmas morning. He pulled on his jeans and a T-shirt and hurried toward the hall. Gene was there, standing in the doorway of his own bedroom, glaring silently. Mason paused. He wanted to show Gene a scary mind picture, but right now he was too excited to concentrate. He'd do it later if Gene did something

esides, Mason was really hungry, so he
_ along the corridor to the stairs, and
em, he ran down.

n his breakfast and saying good-
, who had to "dash to work," Mason
his room. Instead of getting ready for
ol, he recalled the mind picture of the park. Sitting on his bed, he drew the soft, green grass and the blue sky with lots of sunlight. They appeared in the air around him. He imagined the picnic dishes and Rene and Lightning, and Mason settled into the picture, enjoying its warmth and security. For fun Mason thought of a butterfly, and moments later, one flitted through his room, its yellow-and-orange wings slapping at the sunny afternoon air. He laughed and swatted lazily at the bug he'd drawn with his mind.

It was like television, only it was all around him, and Mason could play any picture he wanted. Only hours later, when he suddenly found himself hungry again, did Mason stop his game. He also realized that he'd missed half a day of school, and fingers of fear tickled his belly.

You weren't supposed to miss school. That was bad. Aunt Molly told him so.

Worried about getting in trouble, Mason wasn't quite so hungry, but he fixed himself a sandwich anyway. He ate the meal without tasting it, and the bread and bologna sat in his stomach like a rock. He'd missed school before. He couldn't remember exactly when, but it was the day after Gene punished him that last time. His back had hurt really bad, and he felt sick from it, so he'd asked Aunt Molly if he could stay home, and she said yes. But he hadn't asked Aunt Molly this time, and he wasn't sick at all. Mason put his plate in the sink, convinced that he was in big trouble.

He returned to his room slowly with none of the excitement he'd felt that morning. He shouldn't have missed school. That was wrong, and it made him miserable. He sat on his bed and crossed his legs and gazed at the wall, thinking a mind picture of the park would make him feel better.

But as he conjured the lawn and the checkered picnic cloth, the room remained dark. He was so afraid of getting in trouble for missing school he couldn't bring sunshine to the scene. He placed Lightning on the grass next to his bed, but the dog immediately disintegrated into that other dog—the dark and sick one he'd shown to the ticket taker at the carnival. Mason attempted to bring a butterfly to the scene, but its wings were black and long, and its body grew fat and torn. Instead of a beautiful bug, an ugly crow circled the room, its eyes as orange as flames.

The bird scared Mason, so he stopped drawing the mind picture and fell back on his bed.

When he was a boy—before his mama and daddy went away—Mason had seen the scary birds. His daddy had let Gene use the old toolshed in the backyard as a fort. Gene bought a lock and kept the door fastened all the time, but one afternoon Gene told Mason he wanted to show him something. He'd been excited that Gene would let him into the fort, and Mason imagined they would play cowboys and Indians or some equally fun game. His heart had beat so fast, watching Gene slide a key into the padlock that held the door of the fort closed. His head had been so full of games—and joy that Gene was sharing this private place—Mason was all the more terrified when he finally saw what lay within.

Gene opened the door and pushed Mason into the gloomy shack. The smell was awful. Mason had gotten whiffs of this stink when he played in the backyard, but he didn't think much about it. Now it was everywhere, thick and clinging like syrup—foul, rotten syrup.

Birds and squirrels hung from the walls. The crows had nails driven through their wings so that they looked like they were frozen in the act of flying. Deep cuts in their bellies revealed terrible things. Their beaks drooped to their chests, and black eyes like tiny marbles stared at Mason. The eyes of the squirrels were the same, but their furry little bodies hung above the old workbench, held to the wall with single nails driven through their necks.

Behind him, Gene slammed the door and locked it.

Mason began to cry.

He couldn't remember how long he was trapped in that dim shack with its awful smell and Gene's dead pets, but he remembered beating frantically on the door, begging his brother to let him out. Then he heard the sweet, soft voice of Mama.

"It's my place," Gene protested. "You can't go in there. Daddy promised."

But the door opened and bright sunlight flooded over Mason. Tears had made his sight blurry, but he knew the dark shape standing in the door was Mama, and he rushed to her. She held him tightly and stroked his hair. Mama led him into the kitchen. She used a cool rag to wipe his cheeks and neck and forehead.

Leaving the memory behind, Mason rolled over on his bed and held his pillow. His stomach felt all knotted up and pained from sadness.

That night—the night after he saw Gene's fort—Mason's mama went to the hospital and never came back.

15
Muse

Mason heard about Rene over dinner. He'd seen her picture on TV but didn't really understand what the lady with the pretty blond hair was saying about her. He thought it was kind of neat to see a picture of someone he knew on the television, and he told his aunt Molly all about it over dinner.

"But why is she on TV?" Mason asked.

Aunt Molly looked up from her plate of casserole and shrugged. "Maybe she won a prize," she said. *Please don't let him find out. It'll just crush him.*

Mason took a big gulp of cola and shook his head. "I don't think so. I'd think if she won a prize, everyone would be smiling, but the news lady didn't smile at all. They showed pictures of the woods over to the other side of town and another place I don't know. I wasn't even really paying attention until they showed a picture

124

of Rene, and it was really pretty, but by then the news lady was talking about something else."

"So he knows?" Gene asked as he came into the kitchen, looking like he'd just heard a funny joke. "Good. We really shouldn't try and keep things like this from him. It's counterproductive to his development."

"Gene," Aunt Molly said, startled. "We were just . . ."

"Sad. Sad business." Gene walked around the small table and leaned down, putting his arm around Mason's shoulders. It felt like a crawling snake. "I'm sure Rene will go to heaven, Mason," Gene said.

"Oh now, don't," Aunt Molly protested. "Gene, please."

"She'll be with all the other angels. It's really the most we can hope for."

"Gene! That's enough. You're scaring your brother."

"Rene's not with angels. You only get to be with angels when you die," Mason said.

"Exactly," Gene replied, patting Mason's shoulder and pulling away. He crossed to the refrigerator and retrieved a can of soda, leaving Mason to simmer in fear.

Something bad happened, Mason thought. *Something awful. That's why Rene was on the television.*

Mason shook all over. Aunt Molly reached across the table and patted his hand. She tried to smile, but it looked more like she'd banged her shin on the coffee table.

"Rene was hurt, Mason," Molly said. "That's all. She

just got hurt. She's in the hospital, but she's going to be fine."

"The hospital?" Mason said. People went to the hospital and didn't come back. *Mama. Daddy.*

"She just needs to rest a little. They're taking care of her."

"I want to go," Mason said. "I want to see Rene."

"You can't, honey. Not just now."

"Well, if he wants to see her alive, he'd better get over there quick."

"Gene, I don't want to have to tell you again."

"Otherwise, she's just another angel."

Mason trembled and felt the sting of tears in his eyes. Rene was his best and only friend. Something bad happened. She went to the hospital. People never came back from the hospital.

After dinner Mason paced his room frantically, going back and forth, trying to burn away his concern. The exercise didn't work, though. He still felt frantic. So he sat down at his desk and began to draw, but the pictures all came out dark and terrible. Mason's nerves were so tense, he accidentally snapped his pencil. He opened the drawer of the desk to search for another and came across a set of colored pencils. Aunt Molly had given them to him as a Christmas present. He'd forgotten all about them because he got the gift after

Gene told him to stop drawing.

Using the colored pencils, Mason began drawing the park. He lost himself in the bright hues of green and gold and blue. Whenever something dark and nasty came to his mind, Mason fought it really hard, because the picture had to be nice if it was going to make Rene feel better. The grass spread out on the page with hints of sunlight and shadow on every blade. The river ran in the back, rippling and churning against the far bank. Lightning leaped in the air to catch his tennis ball. People walked or spoke to one another, and everyone was smiling. Mason sat with Rene on a checkered table-cloth, having a picnic. She looked really pretty, just like she did at Frank's, only she wore a white dress, the kind she always used to wear when they were children. In the picture, she laughed and held a big glass of lemonade.

It was a good picture, and Mason would take it to the hospital tomorrow and give it to Rene. She'd like it. It would help her get better.

It had to.

It just *had* to.

16
Grisaille

Mason walked along the outskirts of Marchand, his tennie-runners kicking up bits of dirt and rocks. He'd never gone to a hospital before. He'd seen them on television, on programs where pretty people in white coats talked and joked, but mostly yelled and cried. He knew his mama got hurt when he was a boy. She went to the hospital and never came home. When his daddy got sick, he went to another hospital, and he never came home either.

Mason hoped Rene would come home. He wanted to see her and know she was okay, and he would do it, no matter how scared the hospital made him feel.

Just another angel.

Mason kicked the dirt and stomped forward. Rene said Gene talked like that to be mean because he liked being mean, and Mason thought she was right.

Though it was wrong, and he knew it was wrong, he didn't think he'd mind very much if Gene went to a hospital.

Warm air greeted him when he stepped into the lobby. It didn't look like the hospitals he saw on television. Instead of little rooms with lots of machines shoved in them and people scrunching by one another rushing from one place to the next, the lobby was quiet, with blue sofas and tall, leafy-green plants. It smelled a little like the bathroom at home right after Aunt Molly cleaned it, but there was a sweet smell over that bathroom smell, kind of like bubble gum. The people wore all kinds of clothes, but Mason didn't see a single white coat.

Unsure of what to do, Mason took another tentative step inside, looked around at the sofas and the plants and the hallways and a long desk with an old man sitting behind it. He walked to the desk, and the old man looked up from a book he was reading and peered over the top of his glasses.

"I'm looking for Rene," Mason said, uncomfortable under the old man's gaze.

"Rene?" the man asked.

"Yes, please. Rene. She's my friend."

The old man put down his book and took off his glasses. He smiled a little and leaned closer to Mason.

"Is your friend an employee or a patient?"

"She got hurt."

"Well then," the man said. "That would make her a patient. And what was your friend's name again?"

"Rene," Mason told him. "She's my friend since we were babies."

"Those are the best friends to have. Now tell me, what is Rene's last name?"

"Denton."

The old man nodded. "Let me see what I can find out for you." He lifted a telephone and punched at the buttons.

Nervous, Mason looked at the cover of the man's book. On it, a strange man with a dog's head emerged from a black background, snarling and looking angry. He'd seen this kind of beast before, in movies on the television, but he couldn't remember what it was called. It didn't matter. The picture interested him. Mason's gaze followed the arc of the creature's brow over the points of its ears and down the long, powerful jaws. He noted each tooth, its shape and its sharpness. He observed the color of the eyes—yellow like gold coins— and the tongue—pink and black.

"Son?"

He studied the rounded, muscular chest and the big arms ending in pointy claws. It wasn't a very good picture, not like some he had seen, because the shape didn't look real, and it was supposed to be covered in fur but the hair was drawn badly.

"Son?" the old man said again.

Mason snapped out of his reverie. "Yes, sir?" he asked, having forgotten why he was standing at the counter in the first place.

"Your friend is upstairs. She's in intensive care. You can go up if you like, but you may not be able to see her."

"She's in a tent upstairs?" Mason asked.

The man smiled. "*Intensive care*," he said. "Maybe I'd better show you."

"Thank you," Mason said. You always had to say thank you.

The old man stood. He was taller than Mason and really thin. He walked away and Mason followed, noticing how the man's arms swung when he walked. They turned a corner, and Mason found himself looking at a wall with three elevator doors in it. The old man pushed a button and stepped back.

"Now, when you get inside, press the button with the five on it," he said. "When you get out of the elevator, just walk down the hall to a big counter and tell one of the people there your friend's name. They'll get you set up right as rain."

Right as rain—his aunt Molly said that sometimes, and its familiarity was reassuring. Mason smiled and thanked the man again.

Upstairs, he did what he was told. He stepped off the elevator into a hallway that smelled like the clean bathroom at home, only without the bubble-gum scent over the top of it. And this place did look like the hospitals he'd seen on television.

Men and women, old and young, all in white coats, walked the hall. They didn't even look up at him, but that was fine. He went to the counter like the man told him, and a pretty woman with black hair and green eyes said, "Can I help you?"

"I'd like to see Rene, please. She's my friend, my best friend since we were babies." Mason wanted to say more but stopped himself. He was scared of this place and was worried that he might get in trouble for being here, and the woman with the black hair was looking at him like he'd done something wrong.

"Rene Denton?" the woman asked.

"Yes, please."

"Are you a family member?"

"She's my friend."

"I'm sorry, young man," the woman said, though she didn't look sorry to Mason. "But Ms. Denton can't have visitors just now."

"Oh," Mason said, looking down at the floor. He shoved his hands in his pockets, felt the folded piece of paper with the picture he'd drawn for Rene. Maybe the woman would take Rene the picture. He didn't have to give it to her himself, just so long as she got it. It might make her feel better.

Before he could pull the picture out, a hand fell on his shoulder. Startled, Mason jumped. He turned around and saw Rene's mama and his heart slowed a bit.

"Mason?"

"Yes, ma'am," he said.

Mrs. Denton looked really tired and sad. Her eyes were pink, and her hair didn't look as pretty as it usually did. It was kind of smushed down on one side and really tangly on the other.

"Did Molly bring you out?" she asked, looking around the room.

"No, ma'am," Mason said. "She said I shouldn't come, but I brought Rene a picture to make her feel better."

"That's very sweet," Mrs. Denton said, but she started crying.

"I've already informed the young man that your daughter isn't seeing visitors right now."

"It's okay," Mrs. Denton said, sniffling. "Rene would want to see him."

Mrs. Denton wrapped her arm around Mason's, and the fear he'd felt since walking into the hospital grew worse. It was like Mrs. Denton was really afraid too, and when she touched him, a lot of that fear ran into his body.

"Is Rene okay?" Mason asked.

"We hope so," Mrs. Denton said, squeezing his arm a little tighter. "We're praying."

They walked around the desk, past two men in white coats who were looking at a clipboard and whispering. Ahead of them stood walls of glass with white curtains behind them. The rooms inside were dark except for glowing machines and small lamps. Mason hesitated, feeling as though Mrs. Denton was leading him into the mouth of a monster.

"It's okay," Mrs. Denton said. "You don't have to go in if you don't want to."

But he did want to. That's why he came. He was just being a baby and he knew it. He said, "She's my friend," and they continued to the room.

Inside, Mason saw someone on the bed. It didn't look like Rene, though. A big white cap covered her head, and a square bandage covered her cheek. The other cheek was purple and yellow, the way Mason's arms looked after Gene hit him with the sock. A tube ran over the girl's face, and machines hissed and clicked and beeped around her. But it wasn't Rene. Was it?

"Is that her?" he asked.

"Yes, Mason," Mrs. Denton said, sniffling loudly. She pulled a handkerchief from her pocket and wiped at her eyes and nose. "She was hurt very badly."

"Is she asleep?" he asked. "I don't want to wake her up."

"You can't wake her up," Mrs. Denton said. She started to cry really hard then.

Mason felt responsible. He knew he'd done something wrong, said something wrong, like always. Why was he such a doorknob? Why couldn't he ever say the right thing?

He felt like he might cry too. "I'm sorry," he said.

"It's okay, Mason," Mrs. Denton said through her crying.

But it wasn't and he knew it. He should just leave. Rene wouldn't be able to see his picture anyway, not if she was asleep. He should just give it to Mrs. Denton or tear it up and throw it away.

"Your pictures piss people off," Gene had said.

Looking at Rene, anger joined the fear in Mason's body. Gene lied. People liked Mason's pictures. They told him so. Maybe Rene was asleep and couldn't see the nice picture he'd drawn for her, but he could put that same picture in her mind if he wanted to. If he wished hard enough, he could let her see the park and the river and all of her friends and the sunshine and a nice fried-chicken lunch and big cups filled with lemonade.

Mason gently removed Mrs. Denton's arm from his,

135

and he walked across the room. Closer now, he recognized Rene beneath the bandages and the terrible bruises. He reached out to hold her hand, imagining the perfect Sunday afternoon at their favorite place, wishing she would dream of it until it was time to wake up. He wanted to put his palm on her forehead like his mama had when he felt bad as a boy, but the bandages there scared him. So he slid his hand under hers, really carefully, instead.

Her skin felt warm on his. It was nice, even though he was still frightened. He concentrated as hard as he could on the nice picnic picture; it had to be perfect to make her feel better. But something terrible happened.

The dream of the park and the smiling people and the chicken lunch turned dark as if a sudden thunderstorm rolled in from above. The trees at the edge of the park raced toward him, closing in like an angry mob, and the river slid closer. The grass he'd imagined turned brown and black, melted into leaf-shaped globs. Familiar faces appeared. They were mean and frightening. When the picture finished changing, Mason saw that instead of the park, he was in the Hollow. The faces came closer. And he was scared. So terribly scared.

"Mason?" Mrs. Denton said from the doorway.

He let go of Rene's hand. Sweat poured off his

brow and into his eyes. He stepped away, mouth open, trembling.

"They shouldn't have done it," Mason said, still terrified by the faces in his mind. "They shouldn't have."

"Mason, are you all right?"

He didn't answer. Instead, he ran out of the room, knocking into Mrs. Denton and not even saying he was sorry. And he kept running. He raced down the hall, voices raised at his back. He turned a corner and kept running as if the terrible people in his head were chasing him.

Mason found a stairwell and stomped down it as fast as he could. At the bottom, he threw open the door and sprinted along the hall and into the lobby. The nice old man who had helped him find Rene called out to him, but Mason didn't stop running, not until he was all the way home.

Mason sat on the floor of his room, eyes squeezed tightly against the pain in his chest and his head. He'd never felt so frightened and lost before. Sadness, anger, and fear coiled in his skull and behind his ribs. Usually, when he felt bad, he thought about a nice spring day or playing with his old friend Lightning, or some of his mama's nice chocolate-chip cookies, but none of these familiar comforts helped. Nothing helped.

Mason yanked the paper from his pocket and unfolded it. He stared at the picture he'd drawn for Rene. The park. The picnic. He hated what he saw there. The nice picture was a lie. Rene's picture, the one he'd seen when he touched her hand, was more real.

He stood and carried the sheet to his desk. He slapped the page on the table with the pretty picnic scene facing down. He snatched a black colored pencil from the edge of his desk. Then he started sketching, his hand moving so fast and his fingers squeezing the pencil so tightly that his muscles ached after only a minute. He kept drawing and drawing, though, hoping to get the terrors out of his mind. But even when the picture was complete, and he gazed at the four faces captured on the page, more terrible pictures remained in his head.

The dark and oily thoughts were just too strong to be banished. He pictured the trees of the Hollow, wrapped in the bodies of a thousand black snakes. Not a single leaf or branch or bit of bark was visible beneath the serpents. The ground oozed and pulsed under a blanket of wet, rot-black leaves. Faces floated above the ground. They were terrible faces, twisted up with ugly smiles and hateful frowns. Their mouths moved. They yelled. They laughed. Each movement of their lips brought another flash of pain, another layer of fear.

"Stop it," Mason whimpered into the room.

More creatures appeared in his vision. A great flock of crows with ember-orange eyes and shredded feathers flew through the black woods to perch on the moving branches. Their bellies were opened; bits of their insides poked out and dangled above the dark forest floor. Dogs, similarly abused and long rotted, emerged from among the tree trunks, forming a grotesque pack behind the hovering faces. Black shapes, creatures Mason was unable to fully imagine, slunk in the shadows and clutched at the serpent-ringed trees.

It was all so awful. Mason couldn't take any more of it, so he opened his eyes.

But the haunted forest did not vanish when his eyelids parted. It remained all around him. The walls and floor and ceiling of his room were gone. The woods rolled out ahead of him, seemingly endless, and Mason was trapped with the beasts it harbored.

His fear ticked up a notch. The trembling in Mason's body turned into an audible hum that settled in his head. And beneath this droning, his anger and dread subsided as the thrumming buzz grew louder. A crow flapped its wings, rose from a branch, and then settled back to its perch. The terrible pack of dogs watched him with cold, black eyes. The hum followed his veins from his head to his feet, wiping out all sensation as it went, leaving Mason numb.

A figure in white appeared behind the pack of dogs.

It was Rene, and she looked pretty in a white dress, but Mason felt nothing about it. He simply watched her.

Rene held out a hand to him. Her body trembled and jerked to the side and a spray of blood flew from her mouth. Another twitch of her form and a wound blossomed on her shoulder. A scarlet blotch stained her white hospital dress.

This terrible dance went on for over a minute, but Mason felt nothing. It was like hearing so many noises all at once you couldn't really hear anything at all. His emotions had grown too strong, too loud. As a result, they canceled each other out.

Mason stood and the vision of the forest flickered, faded, and then vanished. He reached down to the desk and lifted the sheet of paper, looked at the faces there—the faces of Lara Pearce, Lump Hawthorne, Ricky Langham, and Hunter Wallace. He followed the contours of their brows and cheeks and mouths.

He examined every line in the drawing.

And he felt nothing.

17
Negative Space

Lara hadn't felt warm in days. At home, she wrapped herself in a blanket and shivered beneath it, though the furnace pumped more than enough warm air. When outside, as she was now, walking to school, she wore a parka that her dad, Larry, had bought her for a ski trip. The family was supposed to go to Aspen, but the trip had been canceled, like all the family trips had. She shook with cold, barely able to keep her teeth from chattering.

"Why, Lara?" Rene had asked.

The question came back to her like a cold stream, running down the back of her head to trickle along her spine. Lara stopped in the street, only half a block from school. She thought she might cry again. She bit her upper lip and breathed deeply through her nose, trying to remove Rene and her question from her thoughts.

It wasn't that easy. She hadn't stopped thinking about Rene and what had happened to her since that night at the Hollow. If she'd known what Hunter was planning, she never would have made that call. God. She never would.

But she did make the call. And worse. She stood there and watched them hurt Rene and did nothing to stop it. She didn't even protest, and she didn't know why. At the time she had felt Rene deserved her punishment—felt Hunter and his friends had every right to beat her up. But why?

"Why, Lara?"

Lara bit down a little harder on her lip to make sure she didn't start crying. She hadn't talked to Hunter since that night and wouldn't if she could help it. Once she'd thought his bad-boy rep was hot. After what he'd done, she just found him terrifying. She took a step forward, knowing she was already late for her first class. Then she stopped.

A white figure stood behind the Marchand High sign. It was Rene, wearing a hospital gown. Even from such a great distance, Lara could see the red and purple wounds staining her face. Recognizing her friend, Lara gasped and stepped back.

This couldn't be real. She'd called the hospital before leaving for school. Rene was still in a coma. But there she was on the front lawn of the school less than fifty yards away, clear and solid and pointing at Lara.

"Oh," Lara said, the sound catching in her throat.

She considered the possibility that she was seeing a ghost. Maybe Rene had died.

It was too much for her. She couldn't go into that school, not where she and Rene had shared so many memories. She just couldn't.

Heart racing, Lara turned away from the apparition. A car skidded on the road only a few feet in front of her. She was so startled, she thought her heart might stop right then.

When she recognized the driver—Hunter Wallace— she almost wished it had.

"Get in the car," Hunter told her.

"I . . . I'm late for class," Lara said with a trembling voice.

"Screw class. We gotta talk."

"I'm really late," Lara tried.

"Get in."

Lara did as she was told, but she moved slowly. Clutching her books to her chest like a shield, she shuffled her feet through the dirt. She reached out for the door handle and leaped back when the door swung open.

Lara climbed in. She felt like she was lowering herself into a black pit.

"Close the door," Hunter said, revving the engine.

She did as she was told again, and Hunter sped away. Lara looked out the passenger window, saw her school pass on the right. She clutched her books tighter and waited.

"You didn't return my calls, baby," Hunter said. "That ain't cool."

"I've been busy," Lara replied. "A lot of homework."

"Homework," Hunter repeated. He snorted out a low chuckle. "Seems more like you're avoiding me."

"Just busy."

"Yeah, well, I been busy too. Me and the boys been working real hard to make sure our alibis are good and tight. Seems they think someone might start talking."

"Really?" It suddenly went from cold to freezing in Hunter's car.

"I don't s'pose I need to remind you that you set this up."

"I didn't know what you were going to do!" Lara cried, her voice so loud it startled her. "You said we were playing a joke."

"You knew. You knew damn good and true what was going down and you didn't do a thing to stop it. So, baby, that makes you an accessory, and if we fry, *you* fry." Hunter's voice grew calmer as he spoke. "Now, your little friend's takin' a nap and ain't sayin' a word. Nobody's got to worry about a thing. But you go steppin' all righteous and we're going to have a whole lot of worry. And I don't *do* worry. So, I'm going to make it a little easier for you."

Lara shivered, kept her eyes on the trees sliding past the window.

"Maybe you're thinking you can turn some evidence and get off free and clear," Hunter said. "Or maybe you're tellin' yourself that you deserve to be punished so you don't worry so much what the cops do to you. But I swear to God, if you say a word about the Hollow to anyone, what we did to your little friend is going to look like a slap on the ass compared to the pain we bring down on you."

"Hunter," Lara said, unsure if it was a plea or a question.

He slammed on the brakes. Lara lurched forward in the seat, nearly smacking her head against the dashboard. A second later, Hunter had his hand wrapped around her face. He yanked hard so that she was forced to look at him.

"Bitch, I am so *not* joking. You lay it down a few times, and you think that makes us tight? That don't make us shit. I'd throw you out on this street and back over you right now if I wasn't worried about messin' up my tires. You think I'm lyin'? Do you? Answer me. You think I'm lyin'?"

"No," Lara cried. She knew he wasn't lying. Anyone who could do what Hunter did to Rene didn't care about anyone. She knew that. She believed it.

"Good," Hunter said. "Now, you take your ass back to school and you remember that mouth of yours is good for only one thing, and talkin' ain't it."

The insult drove into her. Shame made her blush. It tightened her throat so badly she couldn't speak, but she nodded her head furiously so Hunter would know she meant it.

"Good," he said again. "Now get out of my car. I got places to be."

By the time Lara had walked back to school, she was so upset she disappeared right into the girls' bathroom and sat in a stall, crying for over twenty minutes. Once she was certain the worst of the tears were over, she washed her face and reapplied her makeup. She waited for the bell to announce the end of first period and then slipped into the halls amid her classmates.

Lara kept her head down, books tight to her chest. If anyone asked, she'd tell them she was still totally freaked out and upset about Rene's attack.

Walking through the halls, she got the feeling everyone already knew what she'd done. It made no sense and was so impossible, but she felt their eyes on her: Miranda Bocage with her fake nose and breasts; Tod Crawford (Eric's little brother) with the nest of zits on his forehead; Mark Decouteaux and Susan Melvoin, always looking for someplace to make out between classes. They watched her pass, and they knew what she'd done. Done to her best friend!

Cassie was the worst. She wouldn't even look at Lara when they passed in the halls. Once Cassie caught sight of her, she turned her head, nose slightly raised, and continued on as if Lara were a bum asking for change.

Feeling sick to her stomach, Lara wished she'd just stayed home for the day. She could have pounded a bottle of NyQuil and slept through this terrible feeling.

She stopped at her locker to drop off her English textbook, which she hadn't needed anyway. As she placed the book inside the locker, she noticed the picture of Hunter Wallace taped to the door. She tore it off and crumpled it up. Instead of dropping it on the ground and stomping on it the way she wanted, Lara navigated across the hall through the streams of kids and threw the picture in the garbage can. That was where Hunter belonged. He was a low-life freak who pushed drugs. He wasn't even good in bed. Just another boy. Just a nothing.

Except he was a scary nothing with a gun.

"But I swear to God, if you say a word about the Hollow to anyone, what we did to your little friend is going to look like a slap on the ass compared to the pain we bring down on you."

Lara was halfway back to her locker, kids pushing in

on all sides of her, when she saw Rene again. This time, her friend stood less than ten feet away. Her face was bruised and swollen. Her white hospital gown dripped blood, spattering the floor at her broken, misshapen feet.

Lara screamed and leaped into a group of her classmates.

"What the hell?" a boy said, shoving Lara back to the center of the hallway.

Lara stumbled, nearly fell. She righted herself and again saw her beaten friend. Rene raised a hand toward her, a single finger pointed at Lara's chest.

Oh God, she thought. *She is dead. They killed her. I killed her, and now she's come back for me.*

A small crowd gathered. They whispered. Some showed pity, others amusement. Why didn't they see Rene? They had to see her—her bruised and battered face, her bloody white hospital dress. No one said a word.

This is what crazy does to you, Lara thought.

The apparition of her friend trembled. Rene's head whipped to the side as if struck by an unseen fist. Blood sprayed the locker behind her. Lara slapped her hands over her own mouth so she didn't scream.

Then she ran. Down the hall. Away from the gawking crowd. As far as she could get from her open locker.

Even if she had noticed Mason Avrett floor next to the biology lab with his e wouldn't have given him a second thou

One more class.

Lara just needed to make it through Mrs. Denver's dumb-ass art class. Her nerves were finally settling down after a day of complete stress. Rene didn't appear again, but every time Lara turned a corner or looked up, she expected to see her friend, pointing that finger at her. It wasn't a ghost. She knew that. Lara called the hospital right after history class and was totally relieved to hear that Rene's condition hadn't changed. If she wasn't dead, then she wasn't a ghost.

So what was Lara seeing? Just some weird manifestation of her guilt?

She shifted in her chair and looked out the window at the long lawn running from the school building to the football field. She couldn't focus on the assignment, something about negative space and drawing what *wasn't* there. Concentration was impossible, and it was still so cold. Too cold. She clutched the ski parka around her, wishing she were lying beneath a mound of them.

She looked at her classmates, noticing how they were all drawing something on a sheet of paper. All except Mason.

That was strange. This was the only class Mason had a chance of passing, and he usually got as excited as a puppy when Mrs. Denver gave an assignment. Today though, the big goof had his eyes closed.

He was probably upset about Rene too. She was the only real friend the retard had.

Lara looked away, back to the board, where Mrs. Denver finished drawing a circle. The teacher said something, but Lara wasn't listening. She just wanted to go home and get warm.

She returned her attention to the broad stretch of grass outside the window and gasped.

A girl dressed in white stood against the chain-link fence separating the football field and track from the lawn. Black birds circled the air above her. They dove at the ground and rocketed back into the sky. Circled again. Rene walked away from the fence toward the school. She moved with catlike grace, each step seeming to bring her several yards closer. And the murder of crows followed.

Lara ground her lower lip between her teeth to keep from screaming. She scrubbed at her eyes with the backs of her hands.

Rene crossed the vast lawn in less than a dozen steps. She stood just outside the window, her wounds clear and terrible so close up. The birds were wounded too. Lara saw the gashes in their bellies and across their throats. Their eyes, like tiny bits of flame, flashed orange light at her.

Tears filled Lara's eyes. She swallowed a cry.

Rene lifted an arm and pointed. Her mouth dropped open, revealing the great dark pit of her throat. A black snake slid out of her mouth, coiling as it dropped to the grass. Another snake pushed over Rene's lips and circled up to coil around her head, covering her eyes like a blindfold. Its tail rested on her chin. Rene's head fell back and a flock of black birds soared from her mouth, shooting skyward like a perverse geyser.

Lara screamed. Her reason crumbled. She couldn't look away, and even if she could, the damage was already done.

Watching Mrs. Denver at the front of the class, sketching the assignment on their notepads, no one even noticed Lara trembling in her chair and staring out the window. Only when her screams cut through the sound of pencils on paper, chalk on board, did they take notice.

Then the students reared back in their chairs. Some leaped to their feet. Loudly spoken questions and exclamations of surprise filled the room. They looked at the source of the cries and saw Lara Pearce clutching the edge of her desk, still transfixed by something happening beyond the window. They tried to see what she saw but couldn't. Mrs. Denver raced from the front of the room toward her disturbed student. The entire class was in motion.

All except for Mason Avrett, who sat quietly in his chair, eyes closed and head down.

18
Dark Monochrome

Gene sat in his room with the door locked, as always. On the computer screen a white page with a bright blue border was open. It listed the financial activity for a savings account held by a young man named Wesley Michael Montgomery. According to the digital statement, Mr. Montgomery was doing very well for himself. All deposits. No withdrawals. Gene would have envied Wesley Montgomery if the kid weren't dead.

In fact, Montgomery had hardly lived at all. He died from some respiratory disease only a month after his birth. Gene didn't really care about that. His only interest in Montgomery was the birth certificate filed by the hospital, for which he'd paid a good amount of money. With it, he was able to order a social security number in Montgomery's name. He went on to get a driver's license and a bank account up in Shreveport.

On paper Gene was all but broke, his own bank account holding a couple of hundred bucks. Montgomery, however, was quite well off. In a few years, if all went well, Gene could retire in style if he had a mind to. Gene understood the mistakes many young businessmen made and tried to avoid them. A lot of guys in his line of work spent their money as fast as they made it. No thought for the future, no patience for greater rewards down the road. They drew attention to themselves with fine cars and flashy jewelry, living in homes far too opulent to be explained by legitimate financial means, and people noticed. Cops noticed. The government noticed. From there, any brain-dead doughnut vacuum could build a case against them.

That was why Gene still lived at home. He continued to endure the annoyances of his whiny aunt and the doorknob, because they provided him cover. He needed to be ready for the great, big world.

Six months, he thought. Six more months and Gene Avrett would disappear.

Footsteps in the hall drew his attention from the screen. From the sound of the heavy, plodding steps, his little brother was home. Gene closed the bank-statement window—not that he was worried. Even if Mason got a look at the numbers, they would mean nothing to him.

Gene stood up. He was done with his daily accounting

and wanted to pay his little brother a visit.

It amused him to know his business dealings had inadvertently hurt Mason. So he walked into the hall and wandered down to the small room at the back of the house.

The door was partially open, just a crack between door and jamb. Gene strolled right into the room, to find Mason sitting on the edge of the bed, head down. Afternoon light poured through the window at his back. Dust danced in the thick beam of sunshine, circling Mason's huge head and shoulders.

"Disappointment in the halls of learning today?"

Mason didn't move, just kept his big, dumb face pointed at the floor. Likely the doorknob didn't understand what Gene was asking him.

"Bad day at school?"

In answer to the question, Mason looked up. He glared at his brother with anger, an emotion Gene had never before seen on Mason's face. Though Gene felt the urge to back out of the room, he wasn't going to let his idiot brother intimidate him. Instead, he stared back at Mason and forced a smile to his lips. Something was going on in Mason's head. It showed in his gaze. For perhaps the first time, Mason actually appeared to be thinking, and the thoughts weren't good.

They remained locked in a staring match for nearly a minute. Tiring of the game, Gene turned and left, following the dark hall back to his own room. He closed and locked the door.

No sooner had he killed the screen saver on his computer than the landline rang. Gene lifted the phone.

"Avrett," he said.

"Yeah, Gene? Hey, man, it's Hunter."

"Yes?" Gene said.

"We either got us a major break or just got completely screwed."

"That's a broad interpretation of a single event," Gene said. "What happened?"

Hunter told him about Lara Pearce, the girl who'd set up her friend for the dance at the Hollow. Apparently, she went nuts in art class.

"The ambulance came and hauled her away. It was a total crisis."

"And you're concerned that she might recover sufficiently to expose your involvement."

"Yeah, right. She could go full-on narc. Maybe not for a while. I mean, she was messed up *bad*. But who knows, right? They might give her something to calm her down, and then the bitch could spill everything."

"Well, this is problematic," Gene said, feeling the urge to break something. "I'm not sure you realize the level of my disappointment."

"I know, man. I know. This blows hard. With any luck, the skank will be a total basket case 'til they plant her, but what if she's not?"

"What, indeed."

Despite his calm tone, Gene was already scrambling mentally, calculating the amount of time he would need to escape Marchand. Paper trails would need to be erased, as would a certain young lady named Denton. He needed to clean things up and make a quiet departure.

"So, anyway," Hunter continued, "I thought you should know. It might be a total break for us, but you never know, right?"

"I hardly think you're the sort to get that lucky," Gene said. "I suggest you finish your conversation with Miss Denton, and then have a similar conversation with her unstable friend."

"Yeah, but they're both in the hospital, man. No way I can get in and out without a hundred geeks seeing me."

"Perhaps. But right now, these aren't my problems. If they become my problems, you and I will have a conversation of our own. Can you guess what I'm likely to say?"

"Hey, man, chill. It ain't going to come to that. Okay? Denton's still in sleepyland, and it doesn't sound like she's leaving any time soon. I'll figure something out."

"Sooner would be better than later."

"Yeah, right, man. Yeah, I know."

"Good-bye," Gene said.

He hung up the phone. The urge to hurt and break things was strong in him, but right now was the wrong time to take it out on the doorknob. He certainly couldn't take the chance of venting his frustration on anyone else, not with things so close to exploding in his face.

No. This fury he would have to eat and push low. He had to get out of the house, needed to move to clear his thoughts. He would take a drive through the parish, maybe go up to the city for a night and blow off some steam there. If he didn't put some distance between himself and this town, he would do something foolish.

Gene drove north on the freeway. He was aware of the traffic on the road ahead but little else. As he drove, he went over a mental checklist again and again to make sure he'd left nothing out. Ultimately, he came to the same conclusion he had while on the phone with Hunter: The two girls, Rene and Lara, needed management. They were big question marks, and Gene didn't like question marks.

Lara was the immediate problem. Her breakdown might have been a momentary glitch, a passing nightmare that her doctors were already bringing under control. It was highly unlikely she would slide into the kind of permanent madness that had captured Gene's daddy.

Wouldn't that be a bit of luck, though? Many of his problems would be solved if little Lara went the way of Nelson Avrett.

Gene had been nine years old when his daddy snapped. He remembered the night vividly, and why wouldn't he? It was a turning point. Oh, his daddy had never been exactly right in the head. Not even close. For years Gene had listened to the old man's paranoid stories. His daddy used to believe he could capture thoughts from the people he met. He didn't have to touch them or concentrate. Images just came to him like unexpected memories.

On the night his daddy had snapped, Gene stood in Mason's room, ready to smother his baby brother. Ever since the idiot's birth, Gene had all but vanished in the eyes of his parents. They only had time for Mason, because he was so "special." Standing over his brother's bed, palm clasped over Mason's plump nose and disgusting, drooling mouth, Gene was going to prove that there was nothing special about the little lump of meat. He was just a retard who always got to do what he wanted, who always got the last cookie, the last piece of pie.

Beneath his hand, Mason squirmed and slapped. His eyes widened. Gene watched as the fear in those eyes clouded and began to fade. The lids grew heavy and began to flutter.

Then his father started screaming.

Even now, so many years later, Gene believed he had seen something gathering in the room between himself and Mason. Bits of shadow and light came together in dull forms. He thought he saw a beak and a set of black wings, like one of the crows he kept in his shed in the backyard, hovering over his brother's bed, but the image faded quickly.

His father's cries grew louder and Gene raced from Mason's room, throwing open the door, to see his daddy and mama standing on the landing. His daddy swatted the air like he was under attack, and for a moment Gene thought he saw exactly what his daddy did—the black birds swarming the upstairs corridor. His mama grasped at his daddy's arm, calling his name, trying to calm him down.

Stupid woman should have known better.

Gene saw terror fill his daddy's eyes, like the old man was seeing Death himself riding horseback down the hallway. His daddy spun frantically and collided with his mama. She hit the banister hard, rocked for a moment, and then was gone, disappearing over the rail, screaming like a banshee until her neck snapped on the cold wooden floor below.

The house went silent, but only for a moment—a

life-altering moment. Then Mason began crying in the room behind him, and his daddy's eyes cleared. The old man saw what he'd done. Fresh cries of panic—panic for the real and not the imagined—filled the house, until the cops came to take his daddy away.

After that, Gene took control of his family situation. His aunt moved into the house, but she brought no power with her. Little Mason became his pet and his punching bag, and naïve Aunt Molly believed every story about roughhousing, falling off the jungle gym, and whatever else Gene told Mason to say to explain his endless series of contusions.

She didn't want to know what was really happening. Her denial made Mason's punishment all the easier.

As for his daddy, the old man was brain fried. His visions got worse in the nuthouse, so bad the doctors had him medicated 24/7. Nelson Avrett was never getting out.

Now, if Lara Pearce would show the same consideration, Gene's problems would be lessened. Right now, though, it was still a question mark.

And Gene hated question marks.

19
Depth of Field

Humphrey Hawthorne told people he got the nick-name "Lump" from his sister. One summer afternoon, they were playing in the sprinkler in the backyard to cool off when Betsy pointed at his bathing suit and said he had a lump. From that point forward she called him "Lump." His parents followed suit, though they had no idea about the name's origin, and the name stuck. Because the story was true, no one believed him.

It was one of the many "whatevers" in Lump's life. He didn't mind the name. It was certainly better than Humphrey. But folks could have called him "Bubba" or "Jack" or "Rosebud," for all he cared.

He sat in his car outside one of the nasty shacks that dotted the area of town folks called the Bluffs. The Bluffs rose up on the east side of the river. Amid the pine and fir trees, low-rent country folks lived in homes only a few steps above cardboard boxes. Some of the folks on the Bluffs still used outhouses. Some didn't even have electricity.

A whole lot of them seemed to have the money for meth, though. They wiped their tails with old newspapers, but they could always scrounge up enough green for a rocket ride.

Like the woman he was delivering to.

Lump left his car and walked over the dirt to her shack. He knocked on the ill-fitted door and waited.

The door swung back and Lump winced, not giving a damn if the woman noticed or not. Damn. What a nightmare.

Though not an old woman, she looked old. Her blond hair was thin and wispy, like plucked cotton. She had about three teeth left in her head. That was common enough. Like a twisted tooth fairy, meth collected teeth and slid a bit of euphoria under the pillow in exchange. A blue rag of a T-shirt draped over the woman's belly, just touching the waist of her stained jeans. She looked like a low-rent witch with evil in her eyes.

The inside of the shack was lit by a tall metal pipe with a bare bulb at its end. Cracked two-by-sixes lined the dirt to make a rough floor. Naturally, there was a television in the middle of the room. It was the only real piece of furniture in the place. Like the woman, the shack was loosely held together and dismal in appearance. And that would have been fine with Lump—gross, but fine. Hell, he didn't care what people did to themselves. But across the room, Lump saw the woman's daughter, and a knot of nausea tied in his gut.

The little girl squatted in a corner, one arm over her head like she was expecting him to haul off and crack her one.

That was just messed up. Friends and family should mean something. They should mean *everything*. And here was this meth-head bitch letting her daughter run around filthy and scared and living like a total animal just because Mama wanted a fast ride out of reality. That wasn't right. Not right at all.

"You got something for me?" the woman asked, the words soft and mushy.

"Let's see the money," Lump said.

The low-rent witch dug into her jeans pockets and produced a wad of wrinkled bills. Lump counted them. Satisfied, he held out a tiny Ziploc bag, which she lunged at.

"See ya," Lump said, turning away with disgust. As he spun, he caught a last glimpse of the frightened child across the room. *Someone ought to take that kid out of here*, he thought. *Then they ought to beat the hell out of her mother. It wasn't right to treat a kid that way—not your own flesh and blood.*

It made him think about Tara Mae. She wouldn't give up the booze and smokes the way he told her to. He made damn sure she stayed away from the chemicals, but he'd had no luck at all keeping her off the other stuff. She was taking a lot of chances with Lump's kid, and he didn't like it.

Some things were just too important to screw around with. Family was one of them. Lump would do anything for his family. He'd do anything for his friends. He'd kill for them. He damn near had.

He started his car and backed out of the weed-choked path. He wanted to be away from the broken shack and its human litter. Hopefully, Dusty would get his act together and get back on his route soon. *Where is that guy?* Lump hated dealing with the Bluffers and the outer-parish dregs. He knew his chosen profession wasn't likely to bring him up close to movie stars, but damn . . .

On the main road he tried to put the grim house out of his mind, but the little girl wouldn't leave his thoughts. Lump had a philosophy about such things. A philosophy of friends and family—a philosophy of fences.

He'd carried the philosophy for quite some time, and it served him well when the big, old world turned shades of gray. It was like the thing that went down at the Hollow. He didn't have anything against the

Denton girl. In fact, he liked her quite a bit. She was hot, and she was smart. He might have liked to slide on up close with her, but he *wasn't* close to her. She fell outside his fences. Lump's sister and his mama and daddy were in the fences. Tara Mae was in his fences. Hunter and Ricky were in the fences. Everyone else was outside, and no one on the outside better think about hurting what Lump kept fenced up. It was about loyalty. You had to be loyal or you weren't worth a good Goddamn.

So Hunter tells him Denton is going to be causing some trouble. Major trouble. Bull-in-a-china-shop trouble. Lump doesn't need to ask any questions.

Ricky wanted to know why all the time, but Lump didn't need an explanation, not from a dude in his fences.

He navigated around the corner at the peak of the Bluffs, his headlights cutting chunks out of the darkness. Trees rose up on both sides of him, hurried by as he took the steep hill down.

Now, Lump didn't cotton to the idea of beating up on a girl. Not one bit. That was some cowardly crap if you just went around doing it for grins. But this was business. Hunter's business. Lump's business. And sometimes business got ugly.

There might still be some beating left to do.

That didn't matter. Hunter had been his friend since

they were both dirtying diapers. They used to fish the river together, shoot targets in Hunter's backyard with his daddy's .22. For the last two years, they'd been in business together, and both of them did good with it.

You didn't let anything get in the way of that.

He took the next curve, and the lights of Marchand slid from behind the black sheet of forest. Lump liked the way it looked, as if somebody scooped out a big ol' chunk of star-filled sky and dropped it into a bowl next to the river.

As the lights of the city captured his attention, a chill stream ran over his head. It felt like someone was dripping ice water into his skull, and it trickled along the crease in his brain toward his spine. His shoulders shook hard.

He looked back at the road. The sight of the girl on the dirt shoulder ahead startled him more than the sudden, uncomfortable sensation had. She wore a white dress and walked slowly up the hill. He nudged the wheel to the left to give her more room, and he thought the girl was nuts for walking on a dark road so late at night. He slowed the car and cast a quick glance through the windshield as he drove up beside her.

Lump's breath caught in his throat, and his pulse beat like a drum in his ear.

Even as he recognized Rene Denton's wounded face, he told himself, *It can't be her.*

He punched down on the gas pedal and sped away. The first thing he thought was that he'd lost his mind. He didn't believe in ghosts. His crazy aunt Gladys used to tell him all kinds of stories about lost souls and haunts, and Lump thought it was all crap. So if he wasn't seeing a spirit, he was seeing a hallucination.

The idea didn't comfort him much.

He raced around the next curve and kept the gas pedal down.

Then he saw someone else he recognized.

What the hell is he doing out here? Lump wondered.

Mason Avrett sat on a rock halfway up the hillside rolling in on the left of Lump's car. The big goof had his head down like he was sleeping. He didn't even look up when the headlights of Lump's car fell on him.

Maybe it was another hallucination.

He never came to a conclusion on this point. He didn't have the time.

The crows dove out of the sky as thick as a cloud. They had eyes that looked like tiny flames and beaks like wrought iron. All of the birds were wounded. They should have been dead. Even before the first one hit the windshield, Lump could see the insides hanging out of their breasts. Several of them had heads that flopped uselessly from their thick, black bodies.

Hundreds of the birds filled the night, obscuring

Lump's view of the road ahead. He was screaming at the top of his lungs, and in the moment before the murder of crows hit the glass, Lump took his hands from the wheel and used them to cover his face. He was still screaming and shielding his eyes when the car flew through the guardrail and sailed into the night.

Mason raised his head in time to see the taillights of Lump Hawthorne's car disappear over the edge. Remnants of the mind picture of crows still flitted around the vehicle as it vanished.

A moment later he heard the crash. Metal crumpled and glass shattered. The sounds kept coming as Lump's car rolled down the cliffside.

Mason waited for the explosion. In movies there was always an explosion when a car got wrecked.

But no ball of flame or cloud of smoke rose. Eventually there was just silence.

Mason pulled the wrinkled piece of paper from his pocket. He also pulled out the black pencil he kept there. Pressing the sheet on his thigh, Mason drew over the face of Lump Hawthorne. He made loops and scratched lines, gently so he didn't rip through the paper. In a handful of minutes, Lump's face was blended into the dark forest. His cheek became the trunk of another snake-wrapped tree and his eye was covered with the black body of a wounded bird.

Once the picture was altered, Mason folded it, stood up, and shoved the paper and pencil back in his pocket.

Then he walked home, feeling sleepy and little else.

20

Animation

Mason slept late that morning. Before going to bed the night before, Aunt Molly told him that school was closed because of Rene and Lara Pearce and Lump Hawthorne. That was okay. Mason didn't want to go to school anyhow. He was so tired he didn't think he could get out of bed if he wanted to.

Instead he spent most of the morning sliding in and out of dreams. When a bad dream woke him up, he stared at the ceiling until his eyes grew heavy again. Before drifting off to sleep, he tried to picture something nice, tried to feed his dreams with sunshine and picnics and clean, beautiful places, but he didn't have the strength to hold on to such good pictures; they turned scary and grim behind his eyes.

His last dream on that long morning began with Mason sitting in Rene's hospital room. She was awake and smiling, and her face wasn't hurt anymore. This was the mind picture he gave himself. He wanted it to follow him into sleep, to last. Rene looked nice and happy, and she told him all about the hospital and said she was going home soon.

Though Mason created this picture with bright sunshine pouring through the window to land on Rene's pretty face, the weather outside soon turned dark. Rain poured down, rapping the glass like the claws of a monster wanting to get in. Soon the glum atmosphere crept into the hospital room, dimming the lights. Rene stopped talking and fell back on her pillow. Her wounds returned. Purple bruises. Cuts nearly black for their deepness. Skin swollen and bumpy on her cheeks and forehead. Mason stood from the chair and backed away from the bed until he hit the wall. His arms lifted up above his head like he was waiting for Aunt Molly to take off his T-shirt. Then the room was full of the thunderstorm. Black clouds rolled in, covering Rene and the bed and the ceiling and the walls. Mason tried to leave, wanted to get away from the hospital, but he couldn't move his arms or legs. Sharp pains shot up and down them when he tried. The clouds pulled away from the center of the room and coated the walls like ugly paint. The floor was no longer clean linoleum, but dirt. Mason was no longer standing. He sat on the dirt floor, his arms still restrained above him.

Then the hospital room was gone completely. Mason sat in a dark place with only the glow of a kerosene lamp that sat on a small wooden table.

He was in Gene's shack.

A dozen crows, their wings affixed to the boards with nails, decorated the walls on either side of him. Mason knew that he too was kept in place with nails, driven deep into his forearms. Across the room stood a woman. It was his aunt Molly. He could tell by her hair and her dress. She faced the wall, arms at her sides. To her right, in a corner where the lantern's light couldn't reach, something moved. Feet shuffled through the dirt. The sound of heavy breathing, like whatever it was had just finished a long run, came in quick gasps.

"I'd like to leave, please," Mason said. He was looking at his aunt. She didn't move. Maybe she didn't hear him at all. "Aunt Molly, can you get me down, please? I want to go inside now."

But his aunt didn't move. She kept staring at the wall. Her shoulders shook like she was crying, but Mason didn't hear her cry. He heard the feet and the breaths in the dark corner, but Aunt Molly didn't make a sound.

Really afraid now, Mason tried to pull his arms free, but it just hurt too badly. He began to cry himself, even though he knew only babies cried.

"Please," he said. "I don't like it here."

The sounds in the corner grew louder. The dark seemed to move, like it was breathing in time with whatever it hid.

"It hurts," Mason cried. "Please."

Gene stepped out of the pulsing darkness. Though the monster didn't look like his brother, Mason knew it was. That happened in dreams sometimes.

Gene wore the face of an angry dog with eyes the color of pennies. Thick brown fur swept back from the snout to cover his head. Spit dripped from Gene's sharp teeth.

"The trouble is keeping my pets alive," Gene said, nodding his muzzle at the wall beside Mason.

Mason turned his head, seeing the tortured bodies of the dead crows.

"You've lasted longer than any of the others," the Gene-dog said. "How's it feel to actually be good at something, doorknob?"

"It hurts," Mason whimpered.

"Dear little brother," the Gene-dog said, creeping closer. "Pain is the only thing we have left to feel."

Mason woke covered in sweat and trembling. He jerked his arms up, searching for the holes he believed the nails had left in them, but the skin there was unbroken.

He felt terribly alone as he let his head fall back on

the pillow. He wished Rene was better so they could get ice cream. Maybe if he saw her again, he wouldn't feel so bad.

She might even be awake now!

But Mason didn't think so. She was still hurt. It wasn't fair. *Those bad kids shouldn't-a hit Rene like they did. They shouldn't-a, but they did.*

And they were gonna step up. Someone had to step up.

At the hospital again, Mason stood in the hallway outside Rene's room. He wasn't as afraid this time. Other people were in the room with Rene. She was still asleep, so nobody really said anything. Her friend Cassie was there with a tall boy Mason didn't know. He'd seen the boy at school and he seemed nice, but Mason couldn't remember his name. Rene's mama was there and she was crying again, so Mason waited in the hall. Men and women in white coats walked past him, and he kept his head down.

When Rene's mama came into the hall and saw him, her face twisted up and she hurried to where he stood. "Mason," she said, wiping the tears from her eyes. "What are you doing here?"

"Don't know," Mason said. "Wanted to see Rene, I s'pose."

"Well you have to behave," Mrs. Denton said. "Last

time you scared a lot of people the way you ran out of here."

"Sorry," he said. You always had to say sorry and please and thank you.

Mrs. Denton patted his shoulder and sniffled a little. "I know it's scary here."

"Rene's still asleep," he said. It wasn't a question. He knew she was. He also knew that it wasn't a good sleep. He'd seen her dreams and nobody should have to sleep with those kinds of haunts.

"Yes, she is. But the doctors say she's better. It just may take some time for her to wake up."

"I should have brought an alarm clock," Mason said. "Whenever I sleep too much the clock wakes me up."

Mrs. Denton looked at Mason like he had six eyes. She shook her head and a little laugh jumped from her lips. "I don't think the doctors have tried that yet." Then Mrs. Denton began crying again, really hard.

Mason's stomach knotted up painfully. He didn't know what he'd said, but it must have been really mean for the lady to be this upset about it.

"Sorry," he whispered.

"I'm just so angry," Mrs. Denton said between her sobs. "I want them to catch the bastard who did this, and I want them to hurt him. I want his head broken and his arms broken, and I want him to go through the kind of pain my little girl went through. But it won't happen. Even if they catch him, he'll get a comfortable cell and a new suit and a smart-ass lawyer who'll cut some deal so he only spends a few days in jail. And after all Rene is going through, it's just not enough. It's not justice."

"Someone has to step up," Mason said.

"What?"

But before Mason could try to explain the phrase, he saw two boys walking across the far side of the ward. Hunter Wallace, with his painted arms, walked ahead of Ricky Langham, who was wearing a light blue shirt over sand-colored trousers. Seeing the boys numbed Mason. He didn't even feel bad for upsetting Mrs. Denton anymore. The emptiness opened up in him and swallowed his emotions and thoughts.

"They must be here to see that Humphrey Hawthorne," Mrs. Denton said with a sniff. "I hate to say such a thing, but that boy got what was coming to him. Do you know they found drugs in his car? And he's already got himself a baby on the way with that Holloway girl. My heart aches for his mama, it surely does, but he's been playing with the devil his whole life, and he was bound to lose sometime."

"S'pose," Mason said distantly.

He was watching the two boys from school. The hole behind his ribs grew deeper and darker, as dark as the picture he had drawn with their faces on it. When

Hunter Wallace looked in his direction, eyes filled with hate, Mason just stared back. He wanted to show them something awful, paint a terrible mind picture that would make both of them cry. But he wouldn't do it. Not there.

Not yet.

21

Abstract

wall arump am
wall arump am
L-L-L-L-L-L
Thump-thump.

A heart beat in her head. No, *two* hearts beat. One was just above her left ear. The other was in the back. They thumped noisily, but instead of pumping blood, these hearts pumped pain. Each beat brought a bit more agony with it. And she could see the pain. It was made of light. The hearts beat against her brain and a little more light came with them. It hurt, but she wanted the light. It had been dark for so long, she thought the light might be a good thing, even if it meant enduring this rhythmic misery.

Thump-thump. Thump-thump.

Rene opened her eyes. She saw people, people she

knew she knew, but she didn't remember their names. There was a pretty girl with a handsome boy, and an older woman with an older man. They all seemed very happy. Was it a party?

Thump-thump. Thump-thump.

They all started talking, their voices like bits of glass piercing her ears and jabbing at the painful little hearts. They leaned close to the bed, and she saw they'd been crying. But weren't they happy a minute ago?

Oh no, what was wrong? She should ask.

"Wall arump am," she whispered. *"L-L-L-L-L-L."*

Then she returned to the dark for a while, because the light hurt too much.

22
Moving Pictures

"So, who's taking over Lump's business?" Ricky Langham asked from the passenger seat of Hunter's car.

"That's your major issue right now?" Hunter asked.

"We have clients," Ricky said casually. "It's a business."

"And you don't even give a damn Lump's jacked up?"

"When did you grow a soul?" Ricky asked.

"Hey, Asshead, he's been my best friend since we were kids," Hunter replied.

"We've all been friends a long time."

"Yeah, you're some friend. He gets smeared all over a rock and you can't wait to go through his pockets. His face is gone, man. It's just gone. Who knows what the hell is under those bandages? And no way that arm is gonna stay attached. They didn't get it in time. I heard one of the nurses talking. His arm is coming off."

"That blows. But Jesus, it's not like *I* made him go all Dukes of Hazzard and launch his car."

"Maybe you should be thinking more about who did."

You're nuts, Ricky thought. "No one made him. It was an accident. He probably shot a few too many Wild Turkeys before he went out, and he missed the curve."

"It didn't go down that way. I seen Lump down half a bottle and not even blink."

"You're freaked because it happened right after Lara bit the crazy wafer."

"Damn straight," Hunter replied. "That's just too much of a coincidence for my country blood. There were four of us, and now there are two."

"Dude, you said that bitch was about to snap anyway."

"Yeah, and I could buy that just fine, but with what happened to Lump, I don't know."

"Okay," Ricky said, trying to keep from laughing, because Hunter was on the deep end of the paranoia pool. "Exactly what do you think could make her go nuts and send Lump off the road?"

"I don't know."

"Right, you don't know, because the answer is *nothing*. Now, let's figure out how we're going to handle his clients."

"Shut up, Ricky," Hunter warned. "Just shut up."

"We can't just stop."

"God damn it, Ricky, I swear, if you don't . . . What the hell?"

Ricky had been watching the road, an empty stretch of two-lane blacktop running along the river's edge. When Hunter shouted, Ricky turned to him. Hunter's eyes were lit up and crazy. His hands clutched the steering wheel with white knuckles. Then Hunter cranked the wheel to the right, sending them swerving along the shoulder of the road. Ricky was so startled he yelped. Adrenaline pumped fast into his system. He looked around frantically, trying to figure out what was going on. They skidded to a stop.

"Shit," Hunter hissed. "Did I hit her?"

"Hit who?" Ricky asked, his heart thundering in his ears.

"That Denton chick. Did I hit her?"

"What are you talking about? The road was empty."

"She was right there!" Hunter bellowed. He hit the steering wheel with his palms. "She was in the middle of the road."

"Dude, she's in a coma. We saw her mama and daddy crying over her bed an hour ago. There is no way in hell she got up and walked out here."

"She was right there!"

Ricky laughed and shook his head. "Whatever, dude."

Hunter pulled back his fist and drove it into Ricky's shoulder. It wasn't a playful punch but a nasty blow that sent a flare of pain all up and down Ricky's arm. "Damn! Dude, what is your damage?"

"Shut up!" Hunter gave the car some gas and pulled it back on the road. "Just shut up until I get you home. I gotta think."

Ricky rubbed his shoulder and slumped down in the car seat. Dude had no right to haul off and crack him one. What an ass. And what was that crap about seeing Rene in the road? Some kind of mind screw he was playing?

It looked like Lara wasn't the only one who'd taken a bite of the crazy wafer.

Ricky's arm still hurt from Hunter's punch when he let himself into the house. The place was empty and as cold as an icebox. His dad kept the AC cranked 24/7, and heaven help the fool who touched the thermostat. Michael, Ricky's kid brother, still had school. Lump's accident didn't give the middle-school brats a vacation. His parents were still at work. So he had the place to himself for a couple of hours.

He looked around the living room, with its ancient green sofa and doilies covering all the tables, and grunted. The place looked like it belonged to a maw-maw with no taste. Picture frames everywhere. Cheap porcelain statues on the mantel and television. Across the room his mama kept her "valuables" in a wooden cabinet with a glass face. Bits of glass and more pieces of quaint and ugly china. Baubles and trinkets and crap. Nothing more. The stuff in the cabinet couldn't have been worth more than fifty bucks. Damn, he couldn't wait to get out of school, out of the house, and into something with a bit of style.

Ricky firmly believed that he who died with the most toys won. The Bible said the meek would inherit the earth, and that was cool and groovy with him. The meek could eat all the dirt they wanted; Ricky was more interested in plasma-screen televisions and Porsche convertibles. And he'd have those things a hell of a lot faster if Hunter weren't being such a tool.

He rubbed his arm again and headed for the stairs.

It wasn't like he didn't *care* what happened to Lump. They'd been buds for as far back as Ricky could remember. They'd road tripped together and drunk together. At seven years old, Ricky broke his arm falling off the roof while they were hunting squirrels with pellet guns. Lump was there for him. It was Lump who called Dr. Abbott and took Ricky to the office on the handlebars of his bike. When they were nine, Lump showed Ricky his first centerfold in an old issue of *Hustler* from his daddy's stash. So Hunter was totally wrong if he thought Ricky didn't *care*. The fact was, Ricky couldn't *do* anything about what had happened to Lump. He couldn't change it, and he couldn't fix it. So why pitch a fit over it? It happened. It sucked. Move on.

Hunter was seeing conspiracies, and Ricky didn't like it. Hunter was supposed to be managing their business. If he lost it the way Lara had lost it, they could all be in a world of screwed.

Ricky paused at the top of the stairs. A cold tingling sensation started on the back of his neck. He even turned around, because it felt like someone was breathing cold air on him. No one was there, though. Stupid AC.

He walked down the hall to his bedroom and pushed open the door. He thought it might be time to track down the big man—the guy who was really calling the shots.

Hunter made out like he was doing the major deals, but Ricky knew better. Someone else was involved. Someone close. The guy stayed in the shadows, but Ricky had a good idea who was supplying the product. It didn't take a genius to figure it out. A couple years back, he had seen Gene Avrett at Dusty Smith's a few times. At the time, Dusty was handling the high school, and everyone knew that if you wanted anything—weed, crack, meth, smack—you gave Dusty a call. Later that year, Dusty stopped handling schoolyard deals and started selling to the trailer zombies up to the Bluffs. Suddenly Hunter was the guy to call. Out of nowhere,

Hunter had product and cash. And Gene was around. Oh, he never talked to Hunter—or anyone else at school, for that matter—but he was there. Always on the edges. Like a damn rattler waiting to strike.

Ricky needed to set up a meeting with Gene. He needed to let him know that his general, Hunter, was losing it.

Ricky crossed the room to his desk and sat in front of the new flat-panel monitor. He leaned down to hit the computer's power button, and the cold on his neck returned. This time it felt like water—ice water—dripping down his collar. He turned around and froze. He didn't even breathe.

No way.

Rene Denton stood framed in his doorway. She wore a white hospital gown. Bandages were wrapped around her head like a cap above her swollen bruised face. Blossoms of crimson stained the white wrappings over her left ear and at the top of her head. Her mouth opened and closed as if she was trying to speak, but no sound came forth.

Ricky slid his chair back to the desk, where it collided with a *crack*. "You aren't there," he said in accusation. "You're in the hospital."

The girl's mouth dropped open. Broken teeth and a black tongue showed through the gap of her cut lips.

"Crap," Ricky said. "You *can't* be here!"

Despite the cold, a sweat broke out on Ricky's neck and brow. His heart beat so fast he thought it might explode through his ribs. He tried to spin in the chair, but it caught on the edge of his desk. Frantic, he jumped to his feet. He turned to the desk and grabbed a pair of chrome scissors. Brandishing the pointed sheers, Ricky spun back to face Rene Denton.

The doorway was empty.

His throat released a low hiss of air. Thoughts banged and broke in his head. He considered hallucinations and ghosts and dementia, but he didn't believe in any of that crap. No way. Someone was messing with him. He didn't know how, but maybe Hunter was right.

Ricky opened the cell phone he kept clipped to his hip. He looked away from the doorway just long enough to speed dial Hunter, and then he took a step toward the threshold. The Bluetooth headset broke into voice.

"Yeah?" Hunter answered.

"Dude, you were right."

"I'm not laughing, Langham."

"Dude, I'm serious. I just saw Denton in my room."

"If you're yanking my chain . . ."

"Just get over here," Ricky said. "I'm not kidding."

"What was she wearing?"

"What?" Why in the hell would Hunter care about that?

Ricky leaped into the hall, hoping to take his tormentor off guard. He shoved the scissors into the grim air ahead of him as he landed. But the corridor was empty.

"Was she wearing what she had on the other night?" Hunter asked.

"What? No. She was in one of those hospital things."

"Yeah, okay," Hunter said. "That's what I saw too."

"Just get over here, dude."

Ricky continued down the hall, the scissors jutting away from him, ready to stab whatever got in his way. At the top of the stairs, he felt the chill on his neck again and whipped around to find the hall behind him empty.

"Damn," he muttered.

"You see something else?"

The sound of Hunter's voice in his ear startled him. Ricky whirled around and nearly lost his footing. He teetered on the landing for a moment, then threw his arms back to regain his balance. "Crap. I'm hangin' up. I nearly did a header down the stairs. Get over here."

Ricky ended the call and stepped down. *Just get to the*

door, he told himself. *Get outside where people can see you. Everything will be cool if you get out into the sunshine. Ghosts don't like the sun. No, wait, that's vampires. Crap, what difference does it make? It wasn't a ghost. I don't believe in ghosts.*

He took the last step and jabbed the scissors ahead of him as he made the corner into the living room. Rene Denton wasn't there, but he almost wished she were.

Across the room, three dogs stood in front of the door. The animals were big and horrible. They looked dead, except they were standing up, their lips curled back in ferocious snarls. Tufts of yellowish fur stuck out of bodies caked with dirt and blood. Long wounds in their sides revealed grotesque organs, nearly ready to spill out on the carpet. The eyes of the dogs had been damaged—slashed or pierced with a blade. Fluid drained from the sockets.

One of the dogs stepped forward.

Ricky backed away. He waved the scissors as it approached, but it didn't even pause. Its ruined tail, little more than a whip of cartilage with a ragged brush of fur on it, flicked to the side and then tucked low between the animal's back legs. It crouched on the carpet, next to the green sofa. Ricky stumbled back. He shot his hand out for support and drove his scissors through the glass of his mother's curio cabinet. The jagged shards cut the back of his hand and Ricky bellowed in pain. He withdrew the hand quickly. Hurt and irrational, he struck out at the cabinet and sent the light wooden furniture to the floor with a crash.

He didn't wait to observe the damage. Instead, he tore for the stairs, leaping up them two at a time. He ran onto the landing and was struck by another impossible sight. The walls were turning black. The smooth, white plasterboard separated and pulled away into columns that branched out at the top. Tree trunks? Only, these trees were the color of pitch, standing in a black forest atop a carpet of rotted leaves. Things moved over the trees. Black snakes coiled around branches and trunks.

Ricky's throat opened in a deafening scream. He swatted the air with his shears, cut at nothing but atmosphere as he sprinted down the wooded path to his bedroom door, which seemed to stand unsupported in the center of the forest. Ricky hit the door hard, dropping his scissors so he could crank the knob.

Inside, he slammed the door and threw the lock. He looked around his room in a panic, fearing the dogs or the forest had followed him in. But he only saw his familiar and comfortable belongings.

He gasped for breath, working his way from the door

to his window. He lifted the sash and leaned his head out, searching the side yard and the street beyond for any signs of help.

Below, at the edge of his parents' property, he saw Mason Avrett sitting on a tree stump, head down.

What's that brain-dead feeb doing here?

It didn't matter just then. Once he got out of the room and down to the ground, he could pound some answers out of the kid. Right now Ricky needed out. He turned to look at his room again, and was terrified to see black branches poking through the edges of his closed door. A long black snake dripped from the lowest limb, coiling as it lowered to the carpet.

"Oh hell," he whispered.

Ricky pushed the window all the way up and threw a leg over the windowsill. He'd snuck out of the house a hundred times as a kid. It was easy enough. Just climb out and follow the slope of the roof to the eaves, then jump down onto the grass. The only tricky part was getting out of the window, because the ledge was narrow and the fall would certainly cause a hurt if he wasn't careful.

Clutching the window frame with his good hand, Ricky got both feet onto the ledge. He grasped the window tightly and turned to check the slope of the roof. He caught a glimpse of the lawn far below. It seemed so much farther than it had when he was a boy. Ricky tightened his grip on the window frame. He straightened out, turning back to face the house to begin his descent.

Rene Denton's beaten and bloody face hovered an inch from his. Her black mouth with its shattered teeth gaped open. The bandages covering her wounded head slid away, leaving a bloody trail over her scalp.

Ricky screamed at the top of his lungs. He swung out to knock the grotesque apparition away, but his swinging arm passed through the girl. The momentum of the punch tore him from the window and sent him over the edge of the roof. Mind racing, Ricky whipped his arms around, trying to find something to hold on to. His stomach felt like a block of heavy ice. It seemed to fall faster than the rest of him. But he was catching up.

A second later, he landed hard amid a sharp snapping and a deep *whump*! He remained awake, and even thought the fall wasn't so bad. Nothing hurt. He rolled his head slightly and noticed his body was draped over the chassis of his father's lawn mower.

He tried to get up. The pain came to his arms and his neck and his head. Ricky screamed in agony and rolled his head on the grass. Movement made the agony worse, so he lay still and took shallow breaths against the pain.

It felt like he'd been split in half. His upper body sang with misery, but worse than this was the realization that he could feel nothing at all from the waist down.

Ricky looked at the sky, desperation pumping into his blood. Above, a flock of black birds circled like an angry cloud.

23

installation

The day after Ricky Langham fell from his window and broke his back, Hunter woke from a restless sleep. He opened his eyes and looked into the bloody and beaten face of Rene Denton. She hovered over his bed, her nose nearly touching his.

"Shit," Hunter cried, and rolled out of bed. He hit the floor hard, but the ghost of Rene Denton remained before his eyes. He swung his fists. They passed through the phantom. He blinked, but even with his eyes closed, he saw her battered face. He shook his head furiously from side to side until the picture of the girl was gone.

Breathing deeply, he tried opening his eyes again. He did it slowly, testing his field of vision before committing to the act. When he saw the piles of dirty clothes and the discarded magazines, the common litter of his space, he relaxed a bit. Hunter slid his butt over the floor and propped himself against the bed. He rubbed his face harshly to make sure he was good and awake.

Feeling exposed in nothing but his underwear, Hunter stood and pulled his jeans off the bedpost. Sliding them on, he nearly lost his balance. He righted himself in time to see the first of the birds fly through his wall. It was big and black with orange eyes and a long cut in its belly. The crow flew straight for his face. Hunter yelped and fell backward on the bed, but the bird was still in his view. Its sharp beak came right for his eyes. Again he slapped the air, but he missed the attacking crow. Its beak drove into his eye, and then the bird was gone. Hunter threw a palm to his face, realizing quickly that there was no pain.

"What the HELL?" he bellowed.

A moment later, the room was filled with the black birds. Hunter spun in circles, sweeping his arms through the air, trying to bash the crows before they turned on him. But time and again, he missed. His fists hit nothing but air while the birds swooped and circled, crashed into his walls and ceiling. He'd never seen so many birds in one place before. He could hardly see any light between their bodies, couldn't tell where one of the damn birds ended and another began. But they managed to navigate the limited space of his room well enough. They dove for his face and body . . . and passed right through.

And there was something else Hunter noticed. They didn't make a sound. All of the dozens of flapping wings were crammed into his bedroom, and they didn't make a single noise. The only sound came from his chest, and it was a fast, heavy beat.

They aren't real, he suddenly knew. *They're not even ghosts. They're just pictures, like hallucinations.*

"But if I'm crazy," Hunter rationalized aloud, "I wouldn't know it. I wouldn't know I was hallucinating."

He stood upright and let the flock continue its harmless game. He even chuckled when four of the great flying nothings soared through his chest. This was the same kind of thing that had happened to Lara and Lump and Ricky, he thought. Someone was working hoodoo on them, making his friends see things that weren't there. It drove Lara out of her mind and it about killed Lump and Ricky.

But not me, he told himself. *Not me. I know what's real. And this is NOT real.*

As he came to this conclusion, his bedroom door flew open. His daddy, looking like a troll with a hangover, all fat and bearded with eyes so red they could paint a wagon, stomped in. "You want to shut the hell up?" he growled. "As if all of your other crap isn't bad enough, you can't even let us sleep?"

"Whatever," Hunter said, somewhat awed by the sight of the birds passing right through his daddy's body, and his daddy not noticing a one of them.

"Yeah, whatever," his daddy said. "Why don't you go tell that to the cop that's been sitting outside our house all night?"

"Go back to . . ." The sentence fumbled on his tongue. The flock of crows suddenly vanished, and Hunter found himself momentarily stunned by the stillness in the room. "Go back to bed."

His daddy grunted and slammed the bedroom door.

Cops? Hunter thought. *Damn, that isn't good.*

He'd heard the Denton girl woke up. The first reports said she couldn't remember anything about the night Hunter and his boys took her down. He believed it, because if she had remembered, he would be warming a jail cot right about now. But her memory could come back anytime. Or his little girlfriend Lara might come out of her whack and start blabbing.

Hunter crossed to his window and pulled back the shade. Sure as hell, a police cruiser was parked at the curb. No cops were inside it though. Where the hell were they? He leaned closer to the glass, looked down the street. There was the cop, standing on the sidewalk in front of the Porter house. He was talking to Gene's retard brother.

Why's he *here, talking to a cop?*

Damn and damn and damn.

To make matters worse, Gene wouldn't answer his phone, wouldn't respond to emails or IMs. Hunter had been trying to reach him since Ricky took a dive, but Gene hadn't so much as told him to screw off. Gene was totally freezing him out.

After I put the hurt on Denton for him.

"No way," Hunter whispered, letting the curtain fall. "No way in hell."

He was through playing it cool with Gene. He was going to see that bastard and get some traveling cash. Then Hunter was hitting the road for a good long trip.

24
impressionistic

Rene Denton lay in her hospital bed, drifting in and out of sleep. Despite the opiate dripping through her IV tube, there was still a lot of pain. She was awake, though, and that seemed to make everyone happy.

Carefully she rolled her head on the pillow to look at the room. It was depressing. Just machines and wires and tubes. Her mother said she'd be transferred from the intensive care unit to a private room in a day or two.

"There are so many cards and flowers, I don't even know if they'll all fit in it," her mother had said.

The police had come by to talk to her that morning. They wanted her to tell them what had happened to her out at the Hollow, but she didn't remember. She couldn't imagine why she would have been out in the Hollow alone. The last thing she remembered was sitting in a movie theater with Cassie. According to the police, Rene had gone to Frank's with Cassie after the movie. Then she said she was going home for a few minutes, but her mom said she never made it.

Had someone come along and offered her a ride, only to turn violent? Rene supposed it could have happened, but who? She wouldn't have gotten into a stranger's car, and no one she knew would do this to her. Sure, Hunter had threatened her, but she wouldn't have gone anywhere with Hunter, even if Lara was there. Besides, she didn't think Hunter would have let her live if he'd gotten his hands on her.

Her mother had been there all day, fussing and fixing Rene's pillow, offering her sips of water. Right now, her mother was down in the cafeteria getting some lunch, and that was okay. It gave Rene a chance to think a bit without her mother's worried expression floating above her.

wall arump am

L-L-L-L-L

And what was that about? She couldn't be sure. The strange syllables greeted her every time she woke, and they appeared in her thoughts out of nowhere. According to her mother, it was the first thing she said when she woke up, but it didn't make any sense. Rene found the bizarre non-words annoying and wished she could get them out of her head.

wall arump am

L-L-L-L-L-L

Rene rolled her tongue to make the repetitive L sound and smiled lightly. A flash of pain ran through her head, and the smile faded.

She closed her eyes and drifted off to sleep.

It's just a dream, Rene told herself, even as she experienced it.

She stood in the Hollow, surrounded by dark shapes. The shapes had no faces, but they had weapons. Long, thick tree branches dangled from their fists. Everywhere she turned, the darkness moved and writhed like the body of a single great beast. Then a branch cracked against her shoulder and the darkness giggled.

Rene woke with a gasp.

"Oh God," Cassie said, gasping as well. She put a hand over her chest and patted it quickly. "You scared me."

"Sorry," Rene said weakly. "Been here long?"

"About an hour. I came over right after school. Were you having a bad dream?"

"I don't know," Rene said. "I suppose."

"Those are kind of going around," Cassie said.

"What do you mean?"

"Nothing," Cassie said, looking nervous. "Totally nothing."

"Cassie?"

"Look, Rene, your mom would kill me if I upset you. Just forget it, okay? Please?"

"What's going on?" Rene demanded. Even though her voice was weak, it was strong enough to convince Cassie she was serious. "Did someone else get hurt?"

"More than one," Cassie said. "But you can't worry about this stuff. They were accidents, at least Lump and Ricky were."

Lump? Ricky?

"I don't understand."

So Cassie told her what had happened over the last week since she'd been in the hospital. She started with Lara's breakdown, mentioned Lump's car accident and finished with Ricky Langham's fall from a second-story window. Every time Cassie mentioned a name, Rene felt twinges in her mind, like she wanted to remember something, but they passed, leaving her shocked and disturbed.

"Where's Lara now?" she asked.

"Up in the city," Cassie said. "She's at the state hospital. Totally tranq'd."

"Have you visited her?"

"Uh . . . *no*," Cassie said sharply. "God, I didn't want

to see her *before* the meltdown. I certainly don't want to see her in Drooltown. But isn't it weird? I mean, that's like Hunter's whole crowd."

"I wasn't part of Hunter's crowd," Rene reminded her.

"Oh, I totally know. And it's not like they were attacked or anything. Not like you. It's totally different. Just weird."

"Yeah, it is," Rene agreed. "Did anything happen to Hunter?"

"Not yet," Cassie said, frowning. "But we can always hope."

Rene was about to point out that Cassie shouldn't say such a thing, but it required too much effort. And it would have been insincere anyway. She wouldn't wish harm on anyone, but she didn't exactly have to wish it away from them either, especially a cruel boy like Hunter Wallace.

wall arump am

L-L-L-L-L-L

Rene paused. Was that what the first syllable meant? Wallace? She'd always played with words. She mixed them up in her head and played with the syllables. Had she done that in the Hollow?

"I mean, it's not like anyone would care if Hunter got himself injured . . . or deformed," Cassie continued. "It might do him some . . ."

"Shhh," Rene hissed.

Her mind was working over the odd message in her head. If the first part of it was Wallace, as in Hunter, then *arump* might be . . . what?

L-L-L-L-L-L

Larump? she wondered. *Lar-Lump? Lara and Lump?* That left *am. Lam?* It had to be Langham, Ricky's last name. But why were the names of these people mixed up in her head like that? Unless . . .

"Were you at the Hollow that night?" Rene asked. "The night it happened?"

Cassie's face twisted up like she'd just been insulted. "Didn't they tell you? Eric and I found you."

"No one said," Rene responded quietly.

"God, we were, like, right there. We were gathering wood for the pit and we found you in the bushes. It was just awful."

"Were Hunter and Lara there? Were they at Frank's?"

"No. Thank God. That's the only thing that could have made the night worse."

But they *were* there, Rene knew. She remembered nothing about the Hollow, certainly couldn't remember who had met her there, but suddenly, she didn't doubt their guilt for a moment. She had to remember. She had to be sure.

25

Diptych

Hunter wasn't the only one planning to leave town. In fact, Gene Avrett had been making plans for the last two days to do that very thing. He'd wanted to wait until the weekend, but that wasn't in the cards now.

Gene stared at the television set, watching a late-breaking report on the morning news. He balled his hands into fists when the video footage of a familiar house played on the screen. Dusty Smith's body had been found late last night by a neighbor who'd caught a nasty odor while walking through the side yard separating his house from Dusty's place. A video of that very yard played on the screen before the anchorman returned to shake his head somberly in a wholly insincere gesture. Gene fumed.

If that Neanderthal Hunter had been competent, Gene wouldn't have cared about the discovery. But

Hunter failed, and it would only be a matter of time before Denton fingered Hunter and his crew for her assault. Hunter might hang tough. Even if the district attorney offered him a sweet deal, he might keep his mouth shut, but Gene wasn't going to bet his freedom on a *might*. Besides, Denton *might* remember a night not long before her attack when she was walking down Pecan Street, and she happened to see Gene standing on a porch. And oh hey, that just happens to be the house where they found the rotting body of a known drug dealer.

So Gene would go to the bank and close the account he kept under his real name. It wasn't much money, not even a fraction of his assets, but it would get him far enough down the road before he had to worry about going hungry. Gene turned off the television and began packing a small bag with the things he would need for the trip. He carried the bag outside and placed it in the trunk of his car, but he wasn't quite ready to leave yet.

Inside the house, Gene walked down the hall to his brother's room. He pushed open the door and slipped inside. For a moment, he paused to look at Mason's things—the toys on the windowsill, the child's desk with its brightly colored pencil box, the bed where Gene had left the decaying remains of his brother's favorite pet so many years ago. He wished his brother was here, but

Mason had left the house early. Gene wanted to say good-bye, and he had no intention of making it pleasant, but the doorknob ruined that for him too.

Still, Gene knew Mason kept a little money in his dresser. It wasn't enough to fill up Gene's gas tank, but it was Mason's, and Gene wanted it. He crossed to the dresser and pulled open the top drawer. He lifted the neatly stacked T-shirts under which Mason kept his allowance.

Instead of money, though, Gene saw a picture. The paper was nearly black, but at its center three disgusting dog-creatures bared their fangs at him. Gene lifted the sheet and found another gruesome drawing beneath, and another under that. Dozens of the dark and disturbing images greeted his eyes. Each one was so realistically drawn, it might have been a black-and-white photograph, if it weren't for the otherworldly nature of the subjects.

It seemed his little brother was truly losing it. The brat must be eager to follow their daddy to Crazytown.

Good, Gene thought. *Let them lock the little freak up.*

He was replacing the pictures in the drawer when the doorbell rang. Gene's blood raced. His first thought was that the police were wasting no time and had come to ask him questions about Dusty Smith.

Gene crossed the room and leaned over his little

brother's bed to look out the window. There by the curb he saw Hunter Wallace's car, sitting like a tumor on the road.

He wasn't happy to see it. Things were falling apart. The ass had sent a dozen emails, which Gene refused to open. Hunter had been calling his house and his cell phone. The police could trace those calls, and now the idiot was outside.

"You should'a called me back, man," Hunter said, stomping over the threshold past Gene and into the living room.

Gene noted the fury in Hunter's eyes. "What's the problem?" he asked coolly.

"The problem?" Hunter roared. "The cops are sitting outside of my house, and my friends are dropping like flies. How's that for a problem?"

"Keep your voice down," Gene cautioned. "The house is empty, but we do have neighbors."

"I don't really care," Hunter replied. "You sent us after Denton, and now she's screwing with our heads. She's making us see things. She turned Lara's brain to mush and did the same thing with Lump's face. Ricky's paralyzed, man. He's never going to walk again. This morning I woke up and about pissed myself because I saw her in my room, like right over my bed. And then all these birds came in. You sent us after a witch, man. And now you're going to pay up, and I'm getting the hell out of here before she learns some new trick."

Gene couldn't help but laugh. Not because he didn't believe what Hunter had experienced, but because the tattooed idiot had come to such a wrong conclusion.

"She's not a witch," Gene said. "In fact, she isn't even the one doing this."

"The hell she's not. We put a hurt on her, and now she's paying us back."

"It's not her," Gene said. "I assure you."

"Then who the hell is it?"

"Mason," Gene said. His smile faded. "My freak brother is doing this. And if you'll calm down, I'll tell you how. Come upstairs."

Gene handed Hunter the pile of drawings and leaned on Mason's dresser. As Hunter looked through the grim images, Gene remained silent, marveling at the skill—the *only* skill—his little brother had. *What a tremendous gift*, he thought. The pictures themselves were no more harmful than a light breeze, but oh, the damage they caused. Lara and Lump and Ricky could attest to that.

What a perfect weapon. People were slaves to the visual. Movies. Television. The internet. Images were all powerful, and Mason could build any image he chose.

If Gene had been blessed with such a talent, the world would be a very different place. But no, Mason was the privileged one. The brain-dead doorknob, a dolt who couldn't multiply five times five, had been given this extraordinary gift. Of course, the fool was wasting the talent—for a girl. What would you expect? To Mason a cookie was a treasure. A friend who could tolerate his endless ramblings was priceless. Somehow he'd discovered that Hunter and his group were responsible for Denton's attack, and with the ridiculous bravado of immaturity, Mason imagined himself her hero.

"I saw these birds," Hunter said, handing one of the drawings to Gene.

"I thought as much."

"But how's he doing it?" Hunter asked.

"I'll tell you when this is done."

"Oh, it's done," Hunter said. "It's *so* done. I'm out of here."

"Don't be an idiot," Gene said. "Now that we know what Mason is capable of, we can use it. He'll do what I tell him. I'm family, after all."

Hunter returned the pictures to the drawer. He closed it slowly, uncertain.

"Why did you send us after her?" Hunter asked.

"What difference does that make?"

"I want to know. I *deserve* to know, after all of the shit I've been through."

Gene thought about it. He searched for a lie, still unwilling to reveal his crime to Hunter. But instead of a lie, he found a piece of the truth. "Because she liked him," Gene said. He found his jaw tight and anger welling deep in his stomach as he said it. "She treated Mason like he was something special, just like my parents did. She found his stupidity charming. She made him happy, and seeing it made me sick."

"And you wanted her dead for that?" Hunter asked, incredulous.

"Yes," Gene said. And it was as true as his need to have a witness removed.

"That's sick," Hunter whispered. "Damn."

"I have had to sit back and watch the world bend to that bastard's will my entire life. I even tried to kill him myself, because I know what he really is. He is a monster. Plain and simple. I think he's proven that now."

"So, what's the plan?" Hunter asked.

"You find my brother," Gene said. "Tell him you'll hurt Denton if he tries any of his tricks. Take him somewhere quiet. . . . Take him to the Old Bracken Bridge. No one's ever there. You threaten him. Really put the fear of God into the freak. Then I show up and save him. After that he'll do whatever I tell him, even if it means driving Ms. Denton out of her mind. Problem solved."

Hunter nodded his head. Apparently the plan sounded good to him.

Wonderful, Gene thought. Because that wasn't the plan at all.

26
Pentimenti

Cassie was talking about Eric because Rene had asked, but Rene wasn't really paying attention. She'd thought some normal conversation would help alleviate the sense of dread filling her. It didn't. As Cassie described her second date with Eric—"We went to Molina's. It was totally romantic"—Rene thought about Lara and Hunter and the others. She knew they were responsible for her attack, but she couldn't remember them doing it. She didn't even have a flash of memory about it. Certainly nothing she could tell the police beyond a feeling. Still, these were kids she knew, kids from her own school. How could they be capable of something so vicious and hateful? How could Lara?

". . . and he's so sweet," Cassie continued. "I mean, he follows me home in his car, like from school? He wants to make sure I get there safe, and he waits until

I'm inside. Plus, and this is way sweet, we meet every morning for coffee before school, and he knows how I like mine, and he has it waiting for me when I get there."

"It sounds great," Rene said. And it did. She was jealous. All of this time she'd been holding off, waiting for someone perfect. She'd been mourning the loss of Carter Dane, a boy she hardly knew, and she could have died totally alone because of it. Oh, she knew she wasn't totally alone—she had Cassie and other friends from school, and she had her parents—but there wouldn't have been any boy missing her, grieving for her. That struck her as really sad.

"You know Eric's friend Orin?" Cassie said.

"Orin Unger?" Rene asked.

"That's the one. He thinks you're hot. He's, like, totally crushing on you. He was here three times while you were . . . you know . . . before you woke up. He brought flowers."

"He did?" Rene said, surprised. She'd never really given Orin much thought, but hearing that he'd brought her flowers made her feel suddenly close to him. "He's cute," she said, her cheeks blushing.

"He is, right?" Cassie agreed. "We should totally double when you get out of here."

I wish, she thought.

Rene had spoken with her doctors and knew that

weeks, maybe months, of rehabilitation therapy were in her future. Somehow, she didn't think she'd be dating while she was on crutches. That wasn't even the worst of it. The doctors had shaved her scalp to work on her head wound. She had broken teeth and a swollen face that might never heal right. The whole thing just made her want to cry.

Still, she said, "Maybe. That could be fun."

Cassie's face lit up happily. Over her shoulder, a shadow fell on the door frame. Mason walked up to the threshold and looked in sheepishly.

"Hello, Mason," Rene said, glad to see him.

"'Lo," he mumbled.

Cassie spun around, startled, as if she'd been caught saying something bad about Mason. She patted her chest furiously, turning back to Rene with a scrunched, oh-my-God-he-scared-me look on her face.

"Sorry," Mason said, his voice low and sounding depressed. He stepped back, out of the doorway.

"Mason," Rene called. The effort hurt her throat, but she didn't want him to go away. He'd come all the way out to the hospital to see her. Besides, he looked so miserable that she couldn't just let him go.

He poked his head back into the room. "You're talking. I shouldn't-a interrupted."

"You're not interrupting," Rene told him. "Cassie was just going to the caf' for some coffee. Weren't you?"

Cassie looked at Rene and shook her head. "No. Eric is picking me up at one and we're going to lunch. I totally don't want to be jacked up on caff, because I get . . ." Cassie paused when she saw the expression on Rene's face, an expression that said *Get the hell out.* . . . "And I totally need a cup of coffee before I see him, so I'm going to go get one."

"Good idea," Rene said.

Cassie stood from her chair and crossed to Rene's bed. She leaned down and lightly hugged her friend, just putting her cheek next to Rene's. "You're so weird about this guy," Cassie whispered.

"Your coffee is getting cold," Rene replied.

Cassie muttered a "hey" to Mason as she slipped past him into the ward. Mason gave her a somber "'lo."

"Come in," Rene said. "I'm really glad to see you."

Mason looked around nervously, as if frightened and knowing he would soon be attacked but not knowing from which direction the attack would come. He took a hesitant step into the room and then paused. He lowered his head.

"Why don't you sit?" Rene said, lifting her left index finger slightly to indicate the chair.

"I shoudn't-a come."

"Of course you should. It makes me feel better to see you."

Mason looked at her. His eyes lit up for a moment,

but the spark quickly faded. He didn't say anything. He just sat down in the chair and looked at his hands, which he clasped in his lap. Rene was reminded of Mason sitting on the hillside during the carnival, right after that horrible woman had tried to cheat him out of ten dollars.

Her first thought was that he was really worried about her, and she needed to put his mind at ease.

"I'm okay," she said quietly. "You know? I mean it still hurts, and I guess it's going to be rough for a while, but I am okay."

"You're awake," Mason noted.

"Yes. And the doctors said I would be fine."

"I'm glad," Mason said, but he didn't sound glad.

"You don't have to worry about me."

"S'pose."

Maybe Mason already knew she was going to be okay. Maybe something else was bothering him.

"Are *you* okay?" Rene asked.

"I did some bad things," Mason replied, knotting his fingers together tightly. "I thought I was doing the right thing because someone's got to step up, but I don't know. I think they were bad."

"You couldn't do a bad thing," Rene assured him.

"I did," Mason countered. "I hurt them, and I shouldn't-a hurt them, because it's wrong. Just plain wrong. But I couldn't help it."

"Hurt who?"

"Just people."

"Mason, who do you think you hurt?"

"Lara and Lump Hawthorne and Ricky Langham."

wall arump am

L-L-L-L-L-L

Rene felt an electric charge at the base of her neck. She was certain that these were the kids, in addition to Hunter Wallace, who had attacked her. But did Mason know that? How could he? Did he see it happen?

Oh, this is ridiculous, Rene suddenly thought. *How could Mason have done anything to those kids?* Lara lost her mind. Ricky and Lump were in accidents. Mason wasn't involved, but still, he felt guilty. Why?

"Mason, you didn't hurt those people. You may have wanted to, but what happened to them wasn't your fault."

"It was," he said without hesitation. "I showed them pictures, and they were really scary pictures like the one I showed the lady at the carnival."

Rene laughed lightly. The poor kid was just driving himself to distraction with guilt. He'd wished bad things to happen to some folks, and when they did, he felt responsible. She knew she shouldn't laugh, though, and it seemed to upset Mason even more, so she stopped and apologized.

And still she wondered why he had even thought to

hurt Lara and the others. So she asked.

"Because they hurt you," Mason said.

"You saw them?" she asked.

Mason shook his head furiously from side to side. "You showed me."

"What?"

"I came to visit when you were asleep. I drew you a nice picture, but when I tried to give it to you, I saw what happened. And I know what they did, and it made me really mad, and I hurt them."

"What do you mean, you saw what happened?"

"You were dreaming mind pictures."

"And you saw what I was dreaming?"

"S'pose," he said.

No. Rene was not willing to believe this. Mason reading her mind? No way.

"How did you hurt Lara, Mason?"

"I showed her mind pictures."

"Mind pictures?"

"I draw them in people's heads."

"Can you draw me a mind picture?"

"S'pose."

Rene was about to ask Mason to do it when a beautiful golden retriever jumped onto the end of her bed. She recognized the animal instantly as Mason's old pet Lightning. His fur was yellow and white and his tongue lolled from a mouth that appeared to be smiling. Lightning lowered his head to sniff at the sheet and then walked forward, stepping on Rene's broken leg, but she felt nothing.

"Are you doing this?" Rene asked. But when she looked at Mason, his head was down, and he didn't respond. "This is amazing."

Lightning took another step forward, but he began to change. His pretty yellow fur dropped away, leaving black patches of dirt and scab. His teeth crumbled and broke. One of his eyes shriveled up and slid out of the socket.

Rene screamed and the dog vanished.

"Sorry," Mason said, his voice high and frantic. "I wanted to show you something nice, but it turned ugly. Everything turns ugly. I didn't mean to scare you. I didn't mean to."

"It's okay, Mason." Rene's heart beat at a mile a minute. She trembled from the fresh memory of the horrible sight. If what he'd showed Lara and the others was anything like the terrifying dog, she could see how Lump might drive off a road or Ricky might fall out of a window.

It was all grimly fantastic and frightening. Mason's talent was like nothing she'd ever heard of.

"Can you show me what you saw when I was asleep?"

Rene asked. "Can you show me what happened in the Hollow?"

"No," Mason said, shaking his head rapidly from side to side. "No. It's ugly. It's an ugly thing."

"Mason, I need to see it. It will help me remember, and if I remember, no one else needs to get hurt. I can tell the police what happened."

"Am I in trouble?" Mason asked, frightened.

"No, Mason. You're not in trouble. I won't even mention you, but I have to be able to remember what happened. I *need* to remember. Will you help me?"

"S'pose."

Rene watched Mason lower his head. She gripped the blankets tightly with her good hand and prepared for the worst.

Suddenly the room went dark. Around her, shadowy trees rose up from the floor, reaching through the ceiling of her hospital room. Gloom crept over the tiles and the lights there, spreading quickly like liquid. Soon, the ceiling was totally gone and a lace of black tree limbs wove above her. She caught movement on either side of the bed, but Rene could barely turn her head.

Then Hunter Wallace's face formed above her. . . .

"You played the wrong game with the wrong players," Hunter told her.

"Totally," Lara cried happily. "I can't wait to tell everyone at school about the look on your face."

Rene looked at the sickening expression of glee Lara wore.

"Why, Lara?" Rene asked. "How could you?"

Across the clearing, Ricky Langham lifted a piece of burned wood from the ground. In front of her, Hunter's face, looking like a great and evil moon, broke into a smirk. . . . Lump Hawthorne was there too, almost looking ashamed. Almost.

Rene broke to her right. Arms came out at her. She scratched and she kicked, but she wasn't able to get loose.

"Next time," Hunter said, "you mind your business."

Then he swung the thick tree branch. It hit the side of Rene's head, cutting her scalp and sending her sideways into Lump Hawthorne. Her vision blurred. She opened her mouth to scream, but another branch crunched against the back of her head. She dropped to her knees and looked up, pleading.

Hunter swung the branch down on the top of her head. She rocked forward but didn't fall. He brought the club down again and again. The world split apart into a dozen nightmarish frames, one lying over another in a dislocating collage. Then they were kicking her. She watched Hunter's boot pull back and bury itself in her stomach. Once. Twice. Three times. Rene coughed in spasms. . . .

And the mind picture ended. Tears spilled from her

eyes and her body hitched with sobs. She closed her eyes, trying to manage the image Mason had returned to her. Her mind connected the picture to that place in her memory that was wiped away, and other memories flooded back. The fear for her life returned, fresh and scalding. It was all there. The pain. The brutality. It hurt so much, but Rene was also grateful.

Now she could tell the police what she knew. Maybe the others had paid for their pitiless behavior, but Hunter would stand trial. He'd go to jail, though part of Rene wanted him to suffer the way his accomplices had suffered.

Rene sniffled loudly and opened her eyes. She wiped her cheeks, took a deep breath, and looked at the chair. She was about to thank Mason, but he was already gone.

"Thank you," she whispered anyway.

Cassie arrived several minutes later, holding a cup of coffee. As soon as Rene saw her friend in the door, she said, "Give me your phone."

Cassie looked around, surprised. She set her coffee on the chair and reached in her pocket for her cell phone. "What's going on?"

"There's no phone in here," Rene said. "And I need to call the police."

"What did Mason do?" Cassie asked, rushing toward

the bed, clutching the cell phone in her fist. "Did he do something gross?"

"No," Rene said, exasperated. "Mason didn't do anything, okay? He helped me remember. I remember who attacked me. Now give me the phone."

"Well, who did it?" Cassie asked while Rene punched the first digit of the number.

"Hunter Wallace, Ricky Langham, Lump Hawthorne, and . . ."—though she hated to say it—"Lara."

"Oh my, no," Cassie said with a gasp.

"I know. It's totally impossible, but she was there."

"That's not what I meant," Cassie said. She'd never sounded more serious in her life. "I saw Mason in the drive out front. He was getting into Hunter's car."

When the operator came on, asking for the nature of Rene's emergency, she couldn't speak. She just stared at the wall, a wave of fear for Mason crashing over her, making her numb.

Mason?

27

Opaque

Hunter's grip on the steering wheel was so tight his knuckles were white. Thinking about what Mason had done to his friends infuriated him, but it also made him uneasy. All the retard had to do was conjure up one nasty image, and Hunter could lose control of the car, just like Lump. Sure the big idiot would suffer as well, but maybe Mason didn't care much about himself.

"I'm going to tell you again," Hunter said through a tight jaw. "I see one thing that doesn't look right, and my buddy is going to waste your little friend. I don't call him when we get to where we're going, and she's dead. So you just sit there and keep the monsters in your head. You get me?"

That was the lie that got Mason in the car in the first place. Hunter told the dumb-ass kid that he had a friend waiting upstairs and Rene was as good as toast if Mason didn't do what Hunter told him. The threat worked pretty damn good. Hunter took his eyes off the road and looked at Mason. The punk was shaking all over. Hell, he was crying, blubbering like a five-year-old who had broken his trike.

He continued driving north, past the high school on the Old Parish Road. Gene had told him to take Mason out to the Old Bracken Bridge. Nobody lived anywhere close to the place. It was out of the way, and there was a shed Hunter had used plenty of times when he needed some privacy.

"You gonna tell me why you started taking down my posse?" Hunter asked, eyes fixed on the road ahead, tensed for any sudden changes in the scenery. "I mean, we gave you some crap, but you deserved it. So why all of a sudden you go hoodoo freak on us?"

"Someone's got to step up," Mason muttered. He was still crying, so the words broke as he spoke them.

"Yeah, step up for what?"

"You shouldn't-a."

"Oh we *shouldn't-a*," Hunter said mockingly, imitating Mason's tearful voice. "Well, let me tell you something, pudding head. No one tells me what I should or *shouldn't-a* do. No one tells my boys what they should or *shouldn't-a* do, except me. That's a lesson you need to learn."

"You hurt her," Mason said.

"Who? Denton? Damn right we hurt her. But that's nothing compared to what I'm going to do to your sorry ass. You wanna play judge and jury? Well, bring it on."

The one thing he still couldn't figure was how did Mason know what they'd done? Was he there? Did he see it happen? Denton damned well didn't tell him.

Hunter thought about the cop he'd seen that morning. His mind began to race and his panic doubled when he remembered seeing Mason talking to the guy.

"Did you narc me out?" Hunter roared. He pulled the gun from his pants, held it low so it wasn't visible over the dashboard. "*Did* you?"

Next to him, Mason whimpered. Hunter looked over and saw the kid crammed against the passenger door, trying to make himself smaller, like he could avoid a bullet at this range.

"What did you tell that cop?" Hunter insisted.

"Nothing," Mason cried. "Nothing. Nothing. He told me to go home."

"You're LYING to me!"

"I'm not either. I'm not. He told me I shouldn't sit on other people's lawns, and so I should go home, and I was going home, but I wanted to see Rene. I went to the hospital. But I didn't sit on anyone else's lawn. I didn't."

Hunter's rage faded. He almost felt like laughing

as he put the gun between his legs on the seat. This big crying bitch was the bogeyman that had scared his friends into hospital beds? This pudding-headed goof was the mayor of Nightmare Town? Jesus.

"I didn't," Mason whimpered again.

Hunter followed Mason, pushing the idiot along the path. Willows and dogwoods gave way to cypress trees. Tall grasses reached up at them. Nettles and prickly bushes scraped over the denim of their jeans. Ahead, the river roared, turning white and violent in the narrows beneath the Old Bracken Bridge. As they stepped into the flat clearing before the bridge, river spray cooled Hunter's skin, but not his emotions.

The Old Bracken Bridge was made of timbers and long pine railings. Once it had been used to transport lumber from one side of the river to the other, way back when Hunter's pawpaw worked the logs. Now the railings were broken, and the planks of the bridge were rotting out from below. Hunter knew it was still safe to walk on, but no one was going to be hauling a truckload of pine over the Old Bracken again.

The shed stood on the far side. Once it had served as a checkpoint run by the lumber company. But it had fallen to crap. Its boards were warped and shrunk with river moisture and sunlight, so that great gaps appeared between them. The square frame that had once held a window was now empty and crooked.

Beneath the bridge, white water crashed into rocks, sending up ghostly clouds of spray. Tiny rainbows shimmered in the mist.

Ahead of Hunter, Mason stopped, his foot hovering over the first plank of the bridge. He looked back at Hunter with a frightened expression.

"Move it," Hunter said, jabbing his gun into Mason's back.

"Is it safe?" Mason wanted to know.

"Your days of worrying about safe are way behind you, retard. Now get moving."

Mason did as he was told. He walked slowly across the planks, freezing every time one of them squeaked or groaned. Impatient, Hunter pushed the kid forward, making him stumble twice before they reached the far end of the bridge.

"Now, you get in that shack and don't come out until I tell you."

Mason sat on the dirt floor of the shack. It reminded him of Gene's fort, the place he kept his scary pets. This place didn't smell as bad, though. There had been a wooden floor once, he could tell by the jagged bits of wood running around the inside of the frame. It was gone now—just dirt and litter and bugs. But he didn't care about any of that. He only wanted Rene to be okay, and he wanted to be okay himself. He didn't like being afraid. He didn't like the sight of Hunter's gun, because Mason had seen those in movies and knew what they could do.

So he sat on the ground, his finger tracing circles in the dirt. Outside, he heard Hunter talking. Was someone else there? Mason didn't know, but he knew better than to look.

"No, man. We're already here. Where are you?"

As he listened to Hunter's voice, a mind picture began to form. Mason tried to fight it away, but he got the same feeling he'd had at the hospital, when he had to draw what came to him. His finger scratched through the dirt. It wouldn't be a good picture, he knew. His fingers were thicker than pencil points, but it didn't matter.

As he drew, Hunter's voice faded away. Even the loud roar of the river disappeared. Mason heard nothing and saw nothing except for the lines and shapes that emerged in the dirt beneath his finger.

When he finished, Mason looked at the picture, confused. It was just like the one he drew after visiting Rene in the hospital that first time. It had Lara's face, and Lump's and Ricky's and Hunter's. But there was another face, a large face hovering over all the others like a moon: his brother, Gene.

His wonderment over this addition to the image

lasted only a few seconds. With the picture had come a certainty. Hunter and the others had hurt Rene, but Gene was the one who had told them to do it. The mind picture said so, and it had come from Hunter.

This was Gene's fault. Like all of the pain Mason could remember—the beatings, the insults, everything—Gene was the cause. And maybe Gene was coming for him now or, worse, he was going back to hurt Rene again.

Oh no. Oh no.

But with the pleas Mason spoke in his head came the anger and the numbing darkness. They overwhelmed him. The hole opened up in Mason again—deeper and darker than it had ever been before—draining his thoughts and his feelings, leaving only an empty nothingness.

Getting to his feet, Mason pushed open the shack's door with so much force it crashed against the side of the building and sprang loose from its hinges.

Hunter stood ten feet away. He held a cell phone to his ear. He was already reaching for his gun.

Mason created a mind picture and forced it on Hunter. It was nothing more than a black sheet. No elegance or artistry, just darkness.

Hunter cried out and dropped his phone. He was still holding his gun though. He swung it around wildly as he screamed. "I'm blind! You sonofabitch. What did you do? God, I'm blind."

The gun exploded and a piece of wood tore away from the door frame beside Mason's head. Hunter spun and shot again, sending a bullet into the wooden railing of the Old Bracken Bridge. The third shot similarly blew away a chunk of the railing. Hunter spun in circles. His rage and fear flowed out of him with a series of curse words and gunshots. Bullets hit the planks of the bridge, rocks, and dirt as Hunter rocked from side to side, taking aim at any sound.

Hunter turned back toward Mason and fired three more times. Two of those shots punched holes in the side of the shack. The third hit Mason in the shoulder, spinning him around and sending him back into the shack.

The mind picture retreated into Mason's head, but only for a moment. Once the shock passed, he again sent the black sheet into Hunter's mind.

"Stop it," Hunter screamed. "Jesus!"

Hunter spun and swatted at the air, working his way slowly across the Old Bracken Bridge, trying to flee the blindness Mason put in his eyes. As for Mason, he walked out of the shack, not even holding his wounded shoulder. With blank eyes and a mouth set firmly in a frown, he crossed the dirt to the bridge, ignoring Hunter's pleas. He crossed the planks until he stood in the middle of the bridge.

Hunter stumbled. He tripped over a cracked board and hit the railing hard. The board snapped away. Hunter reached out with one tattooed arm. His fingers found nothing to support him and he toppled over the side, plunging headfirst into the vicious river below.

28

Masterpiece

Gene parked behind Hunter's car. He threw a glance up the road and then turned to check over his shoulder. No traffic moved in either direction. He touched the gun tucked in his waistband and set off down the dirt road.

If all went well, Gene would come out of this day free and clear. He'd set Hunter up, and in a few minutes he'd be knocking him down. The guy's incompetence had nearly cost Gene his freedom, and now he had to step up. The story Gene would tell the cops was simple enough—he saw Mason in Hunter's car and followed them to the bridge. Hunter had a gun, which Gene wrestled away from him. In the ensuing struggle, Hunter was shot.

Mason would simply be an innocent bystander, the last victim of Hunter Wallace's killing spree, which had begun with Dusty Smith. Gene figured the cops could put that together easily enough once Rene remembered the night of her attack. Even if she never remembered, Hunter would be the most likely suspect. The cops had already been keeping tabs on him, or so Hunter said.

Easy. Clean. Free and clear.

Gene stepped on a dead branch and the crack startled him out of his thoughts. Ahead, thick bushes and low tree branches blocked the abandoned dirt road. He reached the thicket and pushed his way through. Branches snagged on his shirt and scraped over his cheek. Gene didn't mind. It would confirm to the police how anxious he'd been to rescue his little brother.

A chill rolled down Gene's neck and he paused. He trembled amid the overgrowth and reached for his gun. The plants around him began to shrink and melt. Then the world turned dark.

It happened so quickly that the woods around him might have been nothing more than painted cloth, suddenly yanked away to reveal the gloomy world behind them. Black trees wrapped in writhing snakes stood all around him. The leaves and grass at his feet turned black with rot.

Gene blinked. He rubbed his eyes. Though he knew this change of landscape was his brother's doing, unease seeped over him like cold water. The icy stream spread

over his shoulders and back until it felt as if he were leaning against a sheet of ice.

Then the monsters stepped out of the woods. The dogs came first. Deformed and rotting. Eyes drooping over wrinkled muzzles. Teeth too long to belong to real dogs, bared in rage.

Horrible mutations traveled through the nightmare forest. One creature slithered toward him on legs made of fat snakes. Its torso was that of a man with long muscular arms the color of rotten hamburger meat, and its head was that of a mutilated dog, tongue lolling through teeth as long as steak knives.

Gene knew these things did not exist. They were perverse images spewed from Mason's mind. But they still had an effect. His skin shriveled tightly with gooseflesh and he hurried through the bushes.

When he emerged at the edge of the Old Bracken Bridge, Gene nearly lost his footing; the scene before him was so unnatural that it confused him and threw him off balance.

The black forest ran up to the bridge on the near side of the river and rose from the bank on the far side. The river raced through this nightmare, but the water rushing downstream was crimson. Dozens of freakish creatures like those in the woods flailed and slithered in the water. Thousands of black birds filled the sky. They dove over the treetops and swooped low to the foaming

river. Arcing up, they flew in a high loop before diving again. Gene followed the flock with his eyes. The currents they created in the air were smooth, precise, and hypnotic. Gene felt his stomach roll as if with motion sickness. He closed his eyes for a moment and squeezed the grip of his gun tightly. It seemed the only solid thing to hold on to.

Once his head stopped spinning, Gene opened his eyes and was again drawn to the swooping performance of the birds. Mason stood at their center, leaning on the railing of the bridge, gazing down into the current, which looked like a river of blood.

Gene searched for Hunter amid the trees and Mason's twisted menagerie, but there was no sign of him. Had Mason managed to get rid of him?

Perhaps the doorknob did something right, Gene thought. *That'd be good. One down. One to go.*

He raised the gun. It was time for Mason to step up one last time.

Mason didn't see Hunter fall. He didn't notice the body carried downstream by the current. All Mason saw was a dark forest in which monstrous creatures walked over the ground and clung to the branches of black trees. Blood ran in a thick stream down his arm, but Mason only felt a distant throbbing. The pain was in a different world, like the blue sky and the green trees. Mason

thought that was just fine. Despite the horrible creatures, Mason wasn't afraid of the forest. Here he could see the monsters for what they were. In the other world, they hid until it was too late.

There was no reason to stop the mind picture, no reason to look at the real world at all. Except for Rene.

An explosion sounded and something heavy hit Mason in the back. He was slammed forward against the bridge railing. It creaked against his weight, but it held. Suddenly the dark landscape of his mind picture was yanked away, and he looked down into the white froth of the river. Pain blossomed between Mason's shoulder blades and his legs grew weak. He slipped down the railing and sat on the planks of the bridge, trying to breathe. But every time he inhaled, it felt like someone was stabbing him with glass.

"Doorknob," Gene said, smiling and pointing his gun at Mason. He walked over the planks, shaking his head. "You never learn, do you?"

"It hurts, Gene," Mason said, trying desperately to breathe. Gene would help him. Gene was his brother. They were family, they had to . . .

But no. That wasn't right. Gene was bad. He hurt Rene. Gene had hurt a lot of people. He wouldn't help.

"Well, of course it hurts," Gene replied. "You've been shot."

"Go away," Mason whimpered.

"Why don't you *make* me go away? Why not show me some of your scary monsters and send me away? Oh, I know, because it won't *work* on me! I'm not like Daddy. I don't let stupid pictures control me."

"Just go."

Gene walked up to his brother and knelt down. He put the gun against Mason's cheek, and the scorching metal burned him.

"Ow!" Mason cried.

"You killed our mother," Gene whispered. "Did you know that? It was you. You told Mama and Daddy all about my little hobby with the crows, and that night I decided to see what killing you might be like. It sounded like fun. But you remembered those birds. You made them live again with your damn mind pictures. That's what Daddy was swinging at when he knocked Mama over the banister. He was swinging at the birds you put in his head."

"Mama," Mason blubbered. He wanted her now. He wanted to see her nice smile and smell the sweet chocolate-chip-cookie scent of her. Where was she? Why wouldn't she stop Gene from being mean, like she used to?

Gene stood and brushed at the knees of his pants. "I can't believe you wasted your talent," he said. "The one good thing our daddy gave either of us, and he gave it to

you. Then you wasted it. And for what? Rene Denton? Did you really think she liked you? Jesus, Mason, are you that stupid?"

"Go away," Mason said. His head was growing light. The rush of the river thundered in his ears and the bright daylight burned his eyes. Everything was so harsh and cold. He just wanted to close his eyes and go to sleep.

"Am I losing you, doorknob?" Gene asked, laughing. "You going nighty-night?"

A high-pitched wail rose from the dirt road beyond the brush.

"Before you go, Mason, I want you to know something. I'm not done with Rene Denton yet. Not by a long shot. You take that to bed with you."

Gene turned toward the sound of the police siren. He threw his gun into the river. Looking back at Mason he said, "No gun, no guilt."

Mason heard the car coming up fast. He saw dust rising above the trees to the south. Good. He wanted them to get Gene. They'd stop him from doing anything bad. Wouldn't they?

No gun, no guilt.

Leaves rustled and Mason heard deep voices shouting nearby. He forced himself to look up, and he saw a police officer leaping through the green bushes. The man had his gun drawn, and he was aiming at Gene.

"Step away from him," the officer shouted. "And drop your gun."

Gene Avrett didn't move. "What are you talking about?" he yelled back.

"Get away from that boy and drop your weapon."

"I'm unarmed."

"Drop the weapon!"

Gene looked down and saw a gun resting against his right palm, but he didn't feel its weight. It wasn't real. It was just another picture.

"Wait!" he screamed.

But the officer fired two shots in rapid succession. Both hit Gene in the chest. Stunned, he backed up a step. Then he crashed forward, dead before he hit the planks.

Mason coughed and cried. He couldn't breathe anymore. His body wouldn't work, and that was okay because it hurt so much, and he just wanted the hurt to stop. Someone was talking to him. He felt hands on his face.

"Stay with me," the police officer said. "Hang in there."

But Mason didn't see the man. He saw his mama's face. He saw her nice smile. Her eyes were big and they looked happy, the way they used to when she'd tuck him in at night. Across the bridge, Rene, looking pretty like she always did when he imagined their picnics together, waved at him, but he couldn't raise his arm in reply.

"I'm sleepy," Mason told his mama.

"I'm here," she replied.

Suddenly the scent of sweet chocolate-chip cookies filled his nose, and he knew it was going to be fine. The pain was gone. All of the ugliness was gone. He just saw his mama and Rene and lots of golden light.

"'Night," he whispered, sliding into his mother's arms.

29
Perspective

Rene began her sophomore year at Marchand High School much as she'd begun her freshman year—sitting on the school's engraved concrete sign with a cup of coffee. She watched her classmates file through the front door and was reminded that several other students would not be returning this year. The feeling was bittersweet. All of the hope for the new year was flavored with memories of the last.

After two months in the state hospital, Lara had come out of her breakdown. Rene saw her at the trial—hair long and brushed straight down, the way it had been when they'd first met in the sixth grade. During her testimony, Lara apologized to Rene repeatedly, even when her lawyer objected. Rene cried the way people do when they realize something is lost forever. But Lara told the truth. Her story was exactly like

Rene's. Lara was given two years' probation. The court ordered her to continue therapy until she was eighteen. Ricky Langham went to prison in a wheelchair. Lump Hawthorne might have gone to prison himself, but a catastrophic stroke suffered two weeks after his accident had left him in a coma. Almost a year had passed, and he still wasn't awake.

Hunter Wallace drowned. His body was found wedged against a rock, just where the river took a bend out by the Hollow. The authorities blamed Gene Avrett for his death. Gene was also implicated in the death of Dusty Smith, a known drug dealer and addict, though they never found sufficient evidence to prove his involvement. There was, of course, no doubt that Gene had murdered his brother.

Rene sipped her coffee and slid a finger over her forehead to push back a lock of hair. It had grown in nicely, but she kept it short.

She looked toward the parking lot and saw Cassie walking in her direction. Eric Crawford was next to her, of course. The two had been inseparable since they met. Rene waved and slid off the concrete. They waved back.

Her physical therapy had gone well. She didn't even have a hint of a limp, and for that she was grateful.

Everyone in Marchand speculated on the events of the previous autumn, wondering how so many terrible things could have happened in their town. They couldn't understand what had really happened—not unless they knew about a boy named Mason.

As for Rene, she thought about him every day. But she didn't want to remember Mason in his last days, so sad and confused. She wanted to remember a boy who loved to wrestle with his dog and play tag in the park— a boy who always smiled because he didn't know what lurked in the shadows of the world.

The one thing she would always remember about the last day of Mason's life was the light. Lying in her hospital bed, she'd been terrified for Mason, hoping the police would find him and Hunter before anything bad happened. Her fear had been so great she'd imagined monsters in the room with her—dark, nasty creatures like the dog Mason had shown her. But they were soft and unfocused images, little more than flickering shadows in the gloom. Then a great warm light fell over her. It startled her with its brilliance. After all the fear and pain and confusion, this light seemed to burn the ugly feelings away. It was beautiful and simple, and she knew in her heart Mason had sent it to her.

The light brought a feeling of peace, and she kept the emotion with her. It made the years ahead seem less frightening. Bad things would happen along with the good. Fear and love and anger and joy would be hers. Every moment would be another piece of her.

Some she would toss away and others she would hold close and cherish, like pictures.

Cassie walked up and put her arm around Rene's shoulder. "Think you can handle another year of this place?" Cassie asked.

"I guess we'll find out," Rene replied. But the truth was, she didn't have a doubt in her mind.